Monsters-in-Law
JEANNIN COUNTS

*Pull on your flannel, sip your pumpkin spice latte, turn on
your hoa hoa hoa playlist, and relax into fall for a bit*

One

RAIN PATTERED AGAINST THE taxi window, and I tried to focus on the calming noise. But the blaring horns and my driver yelling at the other cars to "*move already*" broke through the staccato of the weather beating against metal and glass. I sighed. I was going to be late. Again.

Not a very good look for only my second week on the job.

"Hey, pal," the driver said in a thick New York accent, glancing at me in the rearview mirror. "You don't like the way I drive, then you can do it."

I bit back another sigh. I should have taken the subway, but I had snoozed my alarm one too many times that morning, my sink decided to spurt water into my face, and my pants ripped when I shoved my legs into them. Needless to say, I missed my normal train, and instead of waiting for the next one like I should have, I opted to take a taxi. And now here I was, stuck in traffic on a Wednesday morning, debating whether I should text my boss or simply apologize when I walked through the doors.

Deciding on the latter, thinking I could maybe sneak in—an hour late, I noticed with a wince—I sank back into my chair that smelled faintly of urine.

I was definitely going to be fired. This was my dream job too—a journalist position with the New York Times. Why couldn't I get my shit together enough to simply get to work on time? My father would have given me a lecture on time management, whereas my mother would have been behind him saying, "He's just a free spirit. Leave him be."

Free spirit? Not so much. Try spacey. I never seemed to organize my days well, always forgetting important things or getting lost in an unimportant project and losing track of time. Although I'd tried almost every trick I could find on the internet, it was who I was, and I had come to accept that.

Now, if only my boss would take that as an excuse. She was an uptight woman in her mid-fifties who always wore her hair in a tight bun, and I swore it pulled the skin of her face taut. I guess that was one way to save money on a facelift. But it gave her a stern appearance I could imagine finding on any headmistress you would see in a movie. It was all too easy to imagine her snapping a ruler across the back of my knuckles for my tardiness.

I had been living in New York City for the past year after hopping around smaller towns in the South and on the East Coast until a friend I'd met online invited me to visit her in the city. I had fallen in love with it instantly, and she was kind enough to let me stay with her until I was able to get a full-time job and rent my own closet-sized apartment.

When I'd been offered the position here, I was beyond excited. I had always possessed a passion for writing—exposés, specifically—and I had been trying to break into investigative journaling for years.

I suppressed a shiver as the taxi finally pulled in front of my office building, and I thanked the driver quickly while darting out of the car. Drawing my trench coat over my head to keep the rain from wetting my carefully styled, sandy brown hair, I rushed through the front doors.

And straight into somebody walking across the lobby.

My messenger bag flew off my shoulder and skidded across the waxed hardwood floors as I fell backward onto my ass with an *oomph*.

"Oh my God, sir," the man I'd run into said. "I'm so sorry. Are you okay?"

He was sorry? It was definitely my fault.

"Don't apologize," I said. "It was all my..." My words ran dry as I looked up at the most gorgeous man I'd ever seen. He was tall and wore a light blue button-down shirt that clung to his figure. I could see the definition of toned muscles underneath—someone who liked to stay fit but wasn't a bodybuilder. His hair was dark, short, and perfectly styled for work, and he smiled at me with a set of full lips.

Suddenly, a hand was hovering in front of my face, and I gaped at it. The stranger wiggled his fingers as his grin widened.

"Need a hand?" he asked.

"Sure," I said, dazed. "Thanks." Taking his hand—which was warm and soft—he helped me to stand back on my feet. Then he walked over and picked up my bag from where it had slid off to, handing it back to me. I clutched it to my chest. Awkwardness perfused me, and I didn't know what to say. I always seemed to lose my wits when I was around an attractive man.

"I'm Kai," he said.

"I–uh...hi," I said, giving a little wave. "I'm Kai. I–I mean, no, *you're* Kai." This was going fantastically. "I'm Huck."

Kai grinned and, oh no, he had nice teeth.

"Huck," he said, as if he was tasting my name. "Like Huckleberry Finn?"

"Um, yeah, exactly," I said. I rubbed the back of my neck in embarrassment. "My full name is Huckleberry."

"Are your parents big Mark Twain fans?"

"Not exactly. They wanted something that sounded human—" I stopped and choked on my words. "I mean, uh, 'timeless.'"

Get it together, Huckleberry, I chastised myself.

"It's nice to meet you, Huck," Kai said, snapping me back to the present. "I'm kind of new here. It's my first day." He grinned excitedly. "Do you know where Elizabeth Clayton's office is?"

"Oh, yeah, she's actually my boss. We're on the fourth floor. I can...show you if you'd like?"

"That would be great!"

I pointed out where the elevators were, and we started walking toward them.

"I guess we'll be working together, then," Kai said.

My feet chose that moment to collide with each other, and I stumbled. Kai managed to catch my upper arm and keep me from falling flat on my face. I blushed as I mumbled my thanks to him and hurriedly finished walking to the elevator, pushing the button and wishing I could crawl out of my skin.

"Elizabeth is great," I said once we were firmly ensconced within the lift. Light jazz filtered through the tinny speakers. "She can be a bit of a hard-ass at times, but you didn't hear that from me."

Kai laughed. "My lips are sealed."

When we reached our floor, I guided him through the maze of cubicles until we were in my section.

"Huckleberry!" a shrill voice shouted over the din of voices murmuring and phones ringing. I winced. A tall woman marched out of a separate office. Her graying blonde hair was pulled back, and her lips were painted blood red. She wore cats eye glasses, a fitted blouse, a black pencil skirt, and heels that could break an ankle. And she was currently staring at me, tapping her foot, with her arms crossed.

"Yes, Ms. Clayton?" I asked sheepishly, fully knowing why I was in trouble.

"Late again?"

I opened my mouth to apologize and throw excuses at her, but Kai beat me to it.

"Sorry, I think that's my fault," he said. "Huck and I ran into each other"—literally—"downstairs, and I asked him to show me around. I'm Kai Miyashiro, the new assistant journalist."

She pursed her lips and glanced Kai up and down as if weighing the validity of his story. Kai had no idea I was already late before our run-in, but I appreciated him standing up for me. He also didn't know that I was also fairly new here and still within my thirty-day probation period. Too many strikes against me and I'd be out on the streets, living in a cardboard box.

"Fine," she said. "Kai, with me. Huck, get to work."

"Yes, ma'am," we both said at the same time.

Kai and I caught each other's eye as he followed our boss into her office and I slunk off to my desk.

Two

A *THWACK* SOUNDED OFF to my side as Kai leaned against the wall of my cubicle. I jumped at his sudden appearance, clicking out of the website that definitely didn't have to do with work.

No, it wasn't porn. I was just...buying new yarn so I could crochet a blanket. I wanted a different blanket for every season. Spring and summer were done, and now I was moving on to fall. There was a beautiful orange marmalade color that had gotten back in stock recently and—

"Well, she seems *lovely*," Kai drawled, interrupting my thoughts. He was still smiling. I wondered if he ever stopped. If his mouth was capable of forming a frown.

"A peach," I muttered, not wanting others to overhear me. "How did it go?"

"Great!" he said. "She assigned me to work with you to get me up to speed."

I sputtered and coughed, needing to take a long drink from my emotional support water bottle as cover.

"*Me?*" I asked. "I've only been here for two weeks!"

"Huh." Kai shrugged. "Maybe that's why she muttered, 'hopefully that will make him be on time'."

I could feel my cheeks heating, and I ducked my head.

"Do you have a cubicle assigned to you?" I asked.

"Nope. Ms. Clayton said I'm to work here with you until all three of us are comfortable enough that I can be on my own."

Great. Just great. Not only was I on the verge of losing my dream job, but I had yet to even turn in my first article. And now I had to somehow train the most attractive man I'd ever seen while sitting in cramped quarters with him. For an undetermined amount of time.

There was no way this could go poorly.

"Well, pull up a chair," I said.

He did, putting himself entirely too close to me, and plucked up the picture frame I kept on my desk. A small bonsai tree sat nearby, and I was hoping I could keep it alive in this stale environment. The frame had a black-and-white picture of a middle-aged man and woman beaming at each other. The background of trees was tastefully blurred, and the couple seemed genuinely happy.

"Your parents?" Kai asked.

Glancing away from the picture, I said, "Yup." I couldn't tell him it was the picture that came with the frame, and that I didn't have any actual photos of my parents to display. So, I swiftly changed the subject to how he would clock in and out each day.

I spent the rest of the day introducing Kai to our computer systems, where the break room was, and the best times to use the bathrooms. Mike from accounting always came to use ours, for some reason, at 11:30 a.m. each day, and it was generally advised to avoid it for the next thirty minutes. If he sprinted in there, we extended that to an hour.

Then I showed him the best ways to pretend you're working and how Ms. Clayton would come around every two hours like clockwork. You could use the click of her heels as an early warning system in order to appear busy. But I did also show him the things I was researching and some of the articles I'd been working on.

When Kai read through one and told me it was strong writing, I had to glance away to hide my blush.

We even stayed a few minutes past 5:00 p.m. because I could see my boss eyeing me over her glasses. I knew she would judge me if I was an hour late but still left right at close.

Once we were the only two there other than Jessica—the office brown-noser who showed up early and stayed late—I finally started packing up my bag. As we walked to the elevator, Kai grabbed his stomach.

"I'm starving," he said dramatically.

My lips twitched into a smile.

"There's an excellent sushi place only two blocks from here, if you want to get some dinner."

Kai wrinkled his nose. "I actually hate sushi."

Embarrassment flooded me, and I stammered out a reply. "I–I'm so sorry. I shouldn't have assumed. That's really terrible of me and, oh my god, I'm so sorry."

I stopped talking when I realized Kai was chuckling. He slung his arm around my shoulders, and my heart skipped a beat. A few inches taller than me, Kai tucked me into his side and gave me a little shake.

"Huck, I'm kidding. I love sushi. But I also love seeing people's reactions to that."

I sighed with relief.

"I am sorry, though," he continued. "If I had realized how stressed that would have made you, I never would have said the joke."

Shaking my head, my lips twitched into some semblance of a grin. "It's fine. It's a good joke." My heart, however, hadn't gotten the memo that it could calm down, and I was quiet until we got into the lobby.

Luckily, the weather had calmed. The sweet smell of rain on asphalt greeted me as we left the building and turned toward the restaurant. I clutched my bag close to my side while we weaved through the throng of New Yorkers heading home after work or finding something to eat. And I couldn't help but sneak peeks at Kai from the corner of my eye. A continuous soft smile graced his face, and I realized I had been staring when he glanced down at me.

He raised a brow in question, and his smirk grew, making me avert my gaze as quickly as possible.

I wasn't sure I'd blushed this much since high school.

The restaurant was bustling with activity. Not too surprising considering the quality of the food, but seeing as it was a random Wednesday night, I was worried we'd have to awkwardly wait for a table. Because this was definitely *not* a date. We were simply two coworkers grabbing a meal after work. But good grief, did Kai have to be so damn attractive?

Thankfully, we were seated in less than ten minutes in a small booth where we faced each other. Kai's long legs spread out on his side of the booth, and our knees brushed periodically, sending little thrills of heat through my skin.

"What do you usually order, Huck?" Kai asked, having to raise his voice over the noise of the space.

"Anything without fish is fine with me," I replied.

He squinted at me in confusion. "You invited me to a sushi place and you don't want fish?"

I shrugged. "You can blame my mother."

"Are you allergic?"

"No, she simply didn't believe in eating fish. Said it was unnatural."

"But any other animal is fine?" Kai's face was scrunched in confusion, and I honestly couldn't blame him. But I couldn't exactly explain the real reason.

"Yes?"

"Weird. But, okay. Vegetable tempura and California rolls, it is."

When the waitress came to our table, Kai ordered for us both in fluent Japanese. The only word I could understand was "sake". She nodded and hustled off, picking up a toy a baby had thrown to the floor on her way back to the kitchen.

"Did you order us sake?" I asked.

"Yup," Kai said, taking a sip of his water.

"We have work tomorrow."

"And?"

"I don't usually drink when I have to work the next day."

"One drink isn't going to get you drunk, Huck. Live a little!"

I couldn't fault his logic and so when the waitress brought us a bottle, one drink turned into two, then three. After that, I lost count. Kai and I spent several hours there in that cramped booth eating, drinking, and laughing.

He told me stories of growing up as a second-generation Japanese-American, and I relayed my experience with a hard-ass father and more of a "hippy" mother. Still keeping most of the truth close to my chest. Because who knew what would happen if I accidentally said it out loud? Best case scenario, people would think I was crazy or imaginative. Worst case, people become terrified of me and cast me out as a freak.

And I was finally somewhere I felt like I belonged, so I didn't want to ruin that.

We stumbled—well, I did; Kai seemed fine—out of the restaurant and onto the street. A giggle broke free when I tripped on a crack in the sidewalk and Kai had to catch me. Again. This was becoming a pattern.

"Shit, Huck," Kai said, holding me upright. "I hadn't realized you were such a lightweight. Do you need help getting home?"

I shook my head, drunkenly pulling out my phone and finding the Uber app.

"They'll get me home," I slurred. "You go ahead."

He rubbed the back of his neck. "I feel responsible now and I want to make sure you get home safely."

I made a vague *pffft* sound and waved my hand at him. "I'm fine."

Kai chuckled. "Sure you are, Berry. I'll just hang out here until your ride shows up."

Nobody had ever called me Berry before. I liked it. A bit too much, if I was being honest with myself.

Once my Uber arrived, I expected Kai to say goodnight and go on his way to his own apartment, but he climbed into the seat next to me. I frowned at him, and he shrugged in response.

"I couldn't help but see your address when you ordered the ride, and I don't live that far from you. So, I figured I'd stay with you, if that's okay?"

It felt like a lie but one with good intentions, so I nodded. Kai's answering grin almost had me melting into a puddle on the floor mats of a stranger's car.

At my stop, we both slid out onto the sidewalk, and my Uber sped off. I looked up at my apartment, dreading climbing all those stairs. Our elevator had been out of service for several months now, and although the landlord kept promising a fix was coming soon, I wasn't holding my breath for it.

"I should make sure you get home safely," Kai said.

"You already have," I said, the haze of alcohol still pleasantly glazing my senses. As if to prove Kai's point, I tripped over the first step leading into my building, and he had to catch me. *Again.*

"Even so…" he said, his words drifting off. At the thought of all those stairs that lay in front of me, and Kai's proclivity for preventing injuries, I allowed him to hold my elbow all the way up to my apartment.

He saw me inside. Helped hoist me into bed and even took off my shoes for me. I might have thanked him, but I passed out before I could remember.

Three

SOMEONE WAS SCREAMING. I pulled myself out of sleep with a groan, only to realize it wasn't screaming. Just my phone alarm telling me to wake up.

Sitting up, I moaned at the pounding in my head and flopped back down onto my pillow. The quick movement made the room spin, and I debated whether I wanted to puke or not. On the one hand, it might make me feel slightly better. On the other, I didn't know if I wanted to move to get into the bathroom.

I flung my hand blindly at my phone trying to silence it. Maybe I could manage another five minutes of sleep before throwing myself together. I *could not* be late two days in a row.

"Turn it off!" a sleepy voice called from my couch.

Heedless of my headache, I bolted upright and finally managed to switch off the alarm. In my little shoebox of a studio, I managed to fit my full-sized bed in a nook carved out from the main space, a loveseat, a practical TV stand that doubled as a bookshelf, and a multitude of plants.

Curled on my tiny sofa, wearing the same clothes as yesterday, was Kai. My head spun from more than just the hangover.

"How...? What...?" Sentences refused to form. Kai sat up and threw his arm over the back of the couch. His hair was deliciously disheveled.

"Did we?" I asked, pointing between the two of us. Horror mounted as I couldn't recall the night before.

Kai's eyes widened. "No!"

Okay, ouch. He didn't have to sound quite so adamant about it.

"No," he said, his voice softening and face relaxing. "Although you were a very cute drunk, I try not to take advantage of people when they're intoxicated."

Wait. He thought I was cute?

I opened my mouth to compliment him back, but my stomach took that opportunity to revolt, and I had to sprint to the bathroom. I was able to lift the toilet seat right before I emptied myself of mostly acid.

A gentle touch on my back eased some of the burning in my throat.

"I'm sorry," Kai said gently. "I would have had you stop at some point if I had known. Next time I'll make sure you don't drink as much."

Next time. My heart soared at the words. Either that, or it was the next round of vomiting.

After Kai forced me to drink some electrolyte water and we both washed our faces and brushed our teeth (Kai used one of my unopened toothbrushes and laid it down on the counter like he'd be back) we ran onto the street to catch the train.

This time, we both made it right as the doors were closing, and we squeezed into the car. Seconds later, we were sitting on uncomfortable plastic seats with dozens of other people also going to work.

We arrived on time and smiled at Ms. Clayton as we walked in. She scowled at us, looking at Kai's wrinkled outfit with a sneer. Her gaze darted between the two of us, silently assessing. But we continued walking to my cubicle and sat down.

I pulled open one of my drawers and popped some ibuprofen in my mouth. I'd forgotten that I had brought my only bottle of medicine to work, so I hadn't been able to take any until then. Ten minutes later and my headache was easing.

Kai handed me a granola bar he had stashed away somewhere, and I ate it slowly. Once my computer booted up, we got to work.

The rest of the day passed by slowly, and I was feeling fairly sluggish, but I was able to show Kai more about the office and our actual work. Teaching him helped me understand my own duties better, and I started working on an article in earnest.

I had gotten so engrossed in diving into the world of a local politician and their corrupt dealings that I hadn't realized it was half past 5:00 p.m. until Kai tapped me on the shoulder.

"I'm heading home," he said. "I'll see you tomorrow?"

Disappointment bubbled in my chest. Was I hoping he'd come home with me again? That was a one-time thing because I was drunk. And it made no sense for it to happen again. He had no clothes at my place. My bed was too small.

Also, we weren't dating, and we barely knew each other.

"Yeah," I said. "See you tomorrow."

Kai grinned brightly at me and walked out of the cubicle. Jessica was the only one left in the office. I could hear her keyboard clacking away at a furious pace on the other side of the space. This once, I would stay later than her.

For the next hour, I researched Steven Podolski—a candidate for US Senator. He'd climbed the ranks within the political sphere swiftly, and many thought he would be making a bid for president in a few years. On the surface, he seemed great. A family man, donated to charities, a charming smile while signing environmental laws. But I had a gut feeling something was off about him. And my gut was rarely wrong.

I knew he was up to something shady, and I *would* figure it out.

Four

THE REST OF THAT week and the next flew by smoothly. Kai and I spent the days together while I trained him, and we'd typically hop down to the deli for lunch. He kept me constantly laughing. I didn't think I'd had this much fun with anyone since I had left home.

On Friday of his second week at the office, Ms. Clayton said Kai had officially passed his training, and she gifted him with his own cubicle. She begrudgingly congratulated me on a job well done, and I couldn't stop beaming for the rest of the afternoon.

Now I only needed to polish my article and present it to her for consideration.

At the end of the day, Kai wanted to go out and celebrate. And because we were both off on Saturday, he said we should go to a club.

I rubbed the back of my neck sheepishly. "I don't know if that's really my scene."

"Come on, Huck," he pleaded, with his hands together and everything. "Try something new."

"Don't you have other friends you'd rather celebrate with? I'm a coworker you only met last week."

"I have other friends, sure. But I want to go with you."

I smiled. I couldn't help it.

Sighing reluctantly, I agreed to go. Kai whooped, jumping up and throwing his hand in the air.

"I don't have clothes for clubbing," I said. Other than my work clothes, I owned eight pairs of pajamas (one for every day of the week plus an emergency pair), two pairs of jeans, one pair of shorts at the bottom of my dresser that I never wore, and four plain black T-shirts. None of that was exactly suitable for a club.

"Come over to my place," Kai said. "I can find you something."

"I don't know if you noticed," I said, grinning. "But we're not exactly the same size."

Throwing his arm around my shoulder again, he beamed down at me with his stupidly perfect teeth. "Oh, I noticed. I'll still find something. Promise."

An hour later, I was gaping at Kai's apartment. It wasn't opulent by any means, but it was at least four times bigger than my own space. Plus, it was decked out in clean, new furniture, a big screen TV, and the kitchen even had an island. An *island*.

"...How?" I managed to eke out the word.

"Huh?" Kai said, sorting through a freaking wall-to-wall closet. I only had a coat rack! He followed my starstruck gaze around his home. "Oh, yeah. My parents are kind of really good at real estate. And I kind of have a trust fund?"

My jaw went slack. "Why are you working at the Times, then?"

"Because I want to," he responded, turning back to the closet.

I cringed thinking about him sleeping on my used furniture. He was accustomed to...this extravagance, and he had spent the night on a love seat I'd bought at Goodwill for twenty dollars.

"Found it!" Kai shouted, pulling something out of his closet.

It only took one look at the garment for me to shake my head. "No, absolutely not. I'm not wearing that."

He held up a shirt that was completely see-through, mostly because it was made only of black mesh, and a small pair of dark leather shorts.

"I've had these shorts since I was in high school," he said. "They don't fit me anymore, so I figure they'll probably work for you."

"The fit isn't the problem! I can't go out in this..."

"Where we're going, you absolutely can."

I stared at him, eyes wide in terror. "Where are we going?"

Shivering, I stood in front of a club, music from the inside already threatening to rupture my eardrums, and stared at the sign that read DIX.

It had taken Kai all of fifteen minutes to convince me to "just try the outfit on" and once I'd put it on, he'd fake swooned onto the couch. So, of course, I would wear it out.

"Is this a gay club?" I had to yell at Kai to be heard. He stood next to me, wearing skin-tight leather pants, an ostentatiously purple crop top, and he'd lined his lashes with black liner. He was...insanely, ridiculously hot.

"Yup!" he shouted back. "Where did you think I was going to take you looking like this? The Ritz? Let's go!"

His hand was warm on my lower back as he guided me past the line of people waiting to get inside. He nodded at the security guard, who merely glanced at us and obviously recognized Kai, because he beamed and let us in right away.

Inside, the lights were low with blues, greens, and purples strobing overhead. EDM music blared from all perceivable surfaces, and a DJ danced in a corner—completely shirtless. Kai led me to the bar that was fully stocked with every alcohol imaginable.

He leaned into my ear so I could hear him over the noise. "Do you want a blow job?"

"What?" I reared back in shock, searching his laughing face and figuring I couldn't have heard him correctly.

Kai grabbed my neck and hauled me back to him, making me shiver. "A shot, Berry! Do you want a blow job shot?"

Oh. "I've never had one." I turned my head so I could speak into his ear. His cologne washed over me, and I wanted to bury my nose in his neck.

But Kai leaned away from me and toward the bartender. I saw his mouth moving, but couldn't pick up the words. Minutes later, the bartender placed two shot glasses in front of us with a healthy dollop of whipped cream on top.

Suddenly, Kai bent over the bar, fitted his mouth over the shot glass, and I watched in awe as he tipped backward, drinking the entire thing in one go.

"Your turn!" he yelled.

Well, here goes nothing. I did the same thing, realizing the alcohol was more sweet than fiery, and that the blow job was actually a very pleasant experience.

Two more shots had me buzzing, a heady warmth underneath my skin that made me smile. Kai grabbed my hand and hauled me onto the dance floor. We stayed out there for hours, dancing and drinking. Sharing small touches.

Kai had such an infectious personality. It seemed almost impossible not to be happy when he was around.

And that feeling tripled when he pulled me off the dance floor into a shadowy corner and kissed me. Stars exploded in a rainbow of colors behind my eyes. Kai tasted like nothing I'd ever experienced, and I could spend the rest of time learning the exact shape of his lips. The kiss lasted for several minutes—languid, not hungry. Then Kai broke away and murmured in my ear.

"Want to get out of here?"

I nodded, and we wound up back at his place. And I have to say, his bed was much more comfortable than mine.

Five

So, Kai and I started dating. Things were casual at first. For a few weeks, we would share longing looks in the break room at work, small brushes of fingers against hands when we went out to lunch, and occasional dinner dates. Most nights, we would end up at Kai's house to watch TV or play card games. Or do...other activities. But we still had our separate lives and apartments—him more so than me.

Kai had friends and family, and although I had moved to New York after staying with a friend of mine, she had since left for California to pursue her dreams of becoming an actress. Other than Kai, I had nobody. I was typically shy and introverted, and preferred to stay home rather than make any effort to find friends. If Kai hadn't interacted with me and pushed me to do things, I'd probably be daydreaming about him at my cubicle instead of actually knowing what he tasted like.

After we had been not-so-casually dating for a month, Kai asked me to be his boyfriend, and I excitedly accepted. I *may* have jumped into him so hard that my skull crashed into the bridge of his nose, making him bleed. I apologized profusely, thinking for sure this would make him change his mind, but Kai simply laughed. After the bleeding stopped, he held a bag of frozen peas to his nose and kissed me deeply.

Three weeks later, I was spending most of my time at his place. Kai had set aside a drawer for my clothes, I had my own toothbrush in his bathroom, and even my season-themed blankets had migrated over, along with some of my plants. His apartment had been pristine before, but now it felt like a *home* with some greenery sprinkled throughout. I learned that Kai was exceptionally good at cooking, and we stopped eating out as often. He loved to sing and shimmy in the kitchen as he cooked for me, and I loved to sit at the island and watch.

Eventually, he asked me to move in with him, and I canceled my lease. It didn't feel rushed. With Kai, everything felt natural. Right.

He was doing well at work, charming everyone with his smile and making small talk. He'd also do the coffee runs whenever anybody even mentioned that they'd kill for a latte.

I turned in my article on Steven Poldoski and beamed when Ms. Clayton said it was "acceptable." It ran on the fifth page.

At the time, I was unbelievably proud of myself. Kai and I went out to celebrate and ate entirely too much ice cream that night.

But when it came time to vote and Podolski won the seat in the Senate anyway, my heart sank a little. Apparently, nobody had read the article. Or, nobody cared. I wasn't quite sure which was worse.

In September, Kai and I had been dating for close to six months when he asked me if I wanted to have dinner with his parents.

We'd been eating at the time, and I almost choked on my pad thai.

"You want me to meet your parents?" I asked.

"Only if you feel comfortable," Kai rushed to say. "They're in the city for business and asked me to meet up with them at their apartment they keep here. And, well, you're my live-in boyfriend, so...they invited you, too."

Kai's parents typically lived in upstate New York. They'd built a real estate empire and had enough money to comfortably live out the rest of their days, but they were, apparently, workaholics and continued to manage their own company. Kai said they'd come to the city periodically on business dealings, but this was the first time they had since we'd been together.

He obviously had a loving relationship with his parents. He talked about them often and fondly, reminiscing about his childhood. I only talked about my parents in vague terms, and Kai—thankfully—didn't pry.

The question had been posed so innocuously, and Kai continued to eat his dinner, seemingly without a care in the world. But I could tell by the set of his shoulders that he was tense. This obviously meant a lot to him, and how could I tell him no?

"I'd love to meet your parents," I said.

Kai's answering grin warmed my very soul. This was obviously the correct answer, but my stomach roiled with doubt. What if they didn't like me? What if I said something stupid—as I was wont to do—and I ruined the entire evening?

What was I going to *wear*?

A week later, Kai buzzed us in to his parents' fancy apartment complex. There was a doorman and everything. I gawked at the extravagance carelessly scattered about the lobby. I wouldn't be able to pay for the paperweight on the entry desk with my entire month's salary.

We walked into an elevator that appeared to be made of pure gold, but logically I knew that wouldn't make sense. And I continued to stare wide-eyed when Kai pressed the button for the penthouse and hovered a card above a touchpad above the numbers.

A *ping* had the elevator doors opening directly into a foyer. The floors and walls were all white marble, with touches of red decorations throughout. The furniture was all ornate and obviously extremely expensive. I suddenly had the feeling that I didn't belong. Kai had bought me a nice button-down shirt and slacks for the occasion, but it felt more like I was playing dress-up.

Kai continued into the space, calling out in Japanese, but paused when he realized I wasn't following him. My feet seemed glued to the floor, and I was fighting the urge to bolt back into the elevator.

He turned, grinning widely at me with soft eyes, and held out his hand.

"They're going to love you, Berry. I just know it."

Intertwining my fingers with his, I began to be slightly more at ease. I took a deep breath as we rounded the corner into a wide-open space. There were floor-to-ceiling windows across from me that gave a panoramic view of the city. The sun was setting over the water, and lights were flickering on. It was gorgeous.

The view had taken my breath away, and I hadn't noticed the rest of the house. I looked now, though, as Kai led me into the kitchen. It was much the same as the foyer—white marble with red accents. A mix of modern touches with what appeared to be Japanese furniture and art. But I was not the one to ask about decor, because I bought all of mine from the five-dollar bin at our local supermarket.

A man and a woman both stood behind the kitchen island, bright smiles on their faces. They appeared to be in their sixties—Kai's dad had completely gray hair, but his mom still had streaks of black. They were both wearing casual clothing that contrasted with the elegant space. Now it seemed Kai and I were *over*dressed.

"Huck, these are my parents—Naomi and Sato. Mama, Papa, this is Huck." Kai smiled between the three of us, ridiculously giddy that we were all in the same space at the same time.

I cleared my throat, and he squeezed my hand in reassurance. "It's nice to meet you both."

"It's so nice to meet you," Naomi said. Her voice was lovely and melodic with only a slight trace of an accent.

"Thank you for coming," said Sato. His accent was slightly thicker than his wife's. I blinked at him because Kai was a spitting image of his father. It was like putting one of those old-age filters over his photo. And I suddenly had an image in my mind of the two of us as old men, sitting in rocking chairs on a porch somewhere upstate, watching the leaves turn color.

I wanted that life. I wanted that life with *Kai*. Grinning up at him, I squeezed his hand back.

We sat around a circular table, eating with silverware that I'm sure cost more than I could imagine, chatting about this and that. Kai and I discussed our work, and his parents talked about their latest deal. It was all extremely pleasant. Naomi had cooked, and now I understood where Kai had gotten his skills in the kitchen. The food was delicious, and I ate two portions.

As the evening was winding down, I shook hands with his parents.

"This was wonderful, Huck," Naomi said. "At some point, we'd love to have your family over as well."

I could feel all the blood draining from my face.

"Mama," Kai hissed. She glanced at him, confused, and he shook his head slightly.

"My, uh, my parents don't live in the States," I said meekly. It wasn't technically a lie.

"Canada?" Sato asked.

"Papa," Kai snapped. "Enough. If Huck wants his parents to join us, he'll let us know. But no pressure, okay?" He glanced at me as he said the last part. I nodded, my eyes glancing at my new patent leather shoes instead of at anyone else.

Kai's arm came around my shoulder, and he leaned into my ear. "Come on. Let's go home."

"It was lovely meeting you," I mumbled. On numb feet, I walked into the elevator. We had an awkwardly silent ride back to our apartment, and once we were inside, I immediately shucked off my fancy clothes, trading them for sweats and one of Kai's shirts.

I could tell he wanted to talk to me. He kept opening his mouth as if he was going to say something and then closing it again.

I *wanted* to talk about it. There was nobody else I could tell, and since moving here, I'd rarely spoken of my parents. We weren't estranged or anything. They just simply *were* strange, and many people wouldn't understand. But if I wanted a future with Kai, it meant laying out everything.

Sitting next to him on the couch, I took Kai's hand in my own and stared into his eyes. He looked back at me with concern, and I decided to tell him something that had been hovering on the tip of my tongue for months.

"Kai, I love you."

His eyes widened. "Really?" Kai whispered, as if he couldn't believe what I was telling him. As if he was shocked that somebody loved him.

Didn't he know *everybody* loved him? That he was so incredibly easy to love, it would have been impossible for me to walk away from him. If anything, I was the lucky one to have him.

I nodded, and he threw his arms around my neck, hauling me into his lap. Burying my face in his neck, I held him tightly. We sat that way for a minute, soaking each other in.

"I love you, too," Kai murmured against my skin.

We pulled apart slightly, and he ran his thumb over my jaw, his gaze following the movement. Then he kissed me, hard and fast. It was as if we couldn't get enough of each other. Couldn't be close enough.

His warm hands were underneath my shirt, fingers skating across my skin. Kai deepened our kiss, and I moaned into his mouth, clutching at him and tugging him toward me. No. I couldn't get carried away. There was something I needed to tell him.

Forcing my lips off him was harder than I expected. "Kai," I said, grabbing his wrists and tugging them away from my body.

With a groan, he dropped his head onto my shoulder. "I need to be inside you," he murmured, and started pressing kisses onto my neck.

My stomach flipped, and I briefly considered waiting until after sex to have this conversation, but no. If I didn't say it now, I might not ever have the courage to do it again.

"Kai." I was more forceful this time, scooting off his lap so I wasn't on top of him. The temptation would be too strong. "I love you, and I can see a future with you, and so I need to tell you something." I fidgeted, twisting the edge of a blanket with restless fingers.

Finally, he registered the seriousness of my tone and words, and he settled into the couch. His gaze filled with concern, and a slight frown tugged at his lips.

"Is everything okay?" he asked. "Oh God, you're not dying, are you?"

"What?"

"Is this like in the movies where people fall in love but one of them has terminal cancer?"

"What?" I repeated. "Kai, no. I'm not dying."

"Oh, thank goodness," he sighed, but his confusion deepened. "What is it then?"

I inhaled deeply through my nose, held it for four seconds, and slowly exhaled from my mouth. It soothed my racing heart and frayed nerves. Kai sat there quietly, understanding that this was something difficult for me to talk about. I would forever love him for his patience with me.

"My parents are kind of...different."

"Okay," Kai hedged.

"It's hard to explain and I don't want you to think I'm crazy." I buried my face in my hands.

Kai gently pried my hands away. "Berry, I'll believe anything you tell me."

"You say that now," I muttered.

The corner of his lip quirked up. "Try me."

Well, he asked for it.

"My dad is a cynocephalus and my mom is a siren," I blurted the words out as quickly as possible. Heat suffused my cheeks and I knew I was turning bright red.

"What?" It was Kai's turn to ask the question with a confused expression.

Another deep breath. "My dad is a cynocephalus. You know the Egyptian god, Anubis?"

Kai nodded.

"Like that. Actually, almost exactly like that. He has the head of a dog, but the body of a human."

"And your mom is...a siren?"

"Head of a human, tail of a fish," I confirmed.

"Huh." Kai's eyes glazed over and he stared over my shoulder, deep in thought. I let him process, hoping he wouldn't think I was crazy. "Okay," he said eventually, sliding his gaze back to mine.

That was it?

"You—you don't think I'm insane? Think I need to talk to a psychiatrist?"

He shook his head. "I mean, I don't know that I'll completely believe it until I see it. You're so...human." Kai gestured vaguely at my body.

I ran a hand through my hair. "I got my dad's lower half and my mom's upper half. Don't ask me about the genetics of that, because I have no idea. But I was the only full human where we were living, and I never quite fit in, so I moved here. Only to find out I don't quite fit in here, either."

"You fit with me, Huck," Kai said, tugging me into his side and dropping a kiss on top of my head. I couldn't help the stupid grin that spread across my face. Damn, I was lucky to have him.

"Would you maybe want to meet them?" I asked quietly. Suddenly, the fraying hem of my shirt was much more interesting than anything else and I fiddled with it nervously.

"I'd love that," Kai responded. "When do you want to go?"

And that was that. The next day, we asked for two weeks off from work, then began packing. I fretted during our preparations because to many humans, I grew up in a land of monsters. Hopefully, Kai could see past it and would still want to be with me after he met my parents and knew where I came from.

Six

"So," Kai drawled, holding a duffel bag at his side in the middle of our living room. "Where *do* your parents live?"

It had been a few days since we'd decided to visit, and I had already sent my mom and dad word that we'd be coming. But I'd been surprised when Kai hadn't asked me a million questions about things.

I had given him a rundown of who my parents were, their appearance, and their personalities, so he could be prepared. Things were already going to be weird enough. But meeting your in-laws who were literal mythological creatures? It added an entirely new level of strangeness, and Kai had kept quiet about it until now.

"It's a little clichéd, but the town is called The Vale. Have you ever watched *Gilmore Girls*?"

"*Have* I?" Kai exclaimed, his eyes sparkling. "Don't even get me started on Rory's taste in men."

I chuckled. "Well, think of Stars Hollow but less...human."

"Like *Halloweentown*?" Kai asked.

"Yeah! That's a great comparison."

"And how exactly do we get there? I'm guessing we can't take the train."

From my pocket, I pulled out a marble-sized orb. It was clear with a golden sunburst in the middle, and I held it up so Kai could look at it. Before he could ask the expected questions, I wrapped the ball in my fist, closed my eyes, and thought of home.

When it warmed my palm, I knew it had worked, and I unfurled my fingers while opening my eyes. It now glowed bright yellow within my hands, and I smiled at Kai's unbridled shock.

"Watch this," I said with a smirk, then I threw the ball into the air in our foyer. It stopped mid-air and hovered, golden light sprinkling down from it. Once the light touched the floor, it spread and connected, becoming more solid on the sides and forming a portal to my home.

The edges glowed brilliantly but the center began to form a hazy image. I sighed in relief when it was the empty forest trail I had been imagining. It was a couple of blocks away from my home, and I thought it'd be better for Kai to walk into things slowly instead of stepping out directly into my parents' living room.

"Come on," I said. With a giant grin, I grabbed Kai's hand and tugged him through the portal.

Autumn was in full swing. Luckily, the weather between New York and The Vale was extremely similar, so we were well dressed. Trees surrounded us as we stood on a wooden walkway. The leaves were colored in russet, orange, and gold. A few fluttered from the branches to the ground and crunched underfoot while we walked. Birds tweeted merrily in the trees, and a few squirrels could be heard squawking in annoyance at our sudden appearance.

"Huck!" Kai exclaimed, making me whip my head to him in alarm and hoping he hadn't somehow gotten stuck in the portal. But he appeared to be whole and overall fine.

"What?" I asked, still concerned.

"Your hair!"

Oh, right. I ran a hand through my typically sandy brown hair, which had since turned a light shade of purple once we stepped into The Vale.

"This is kind of my natural hair color," I said sheepishly. "I normally dye it. Purple might be okay in some professions, but Ms. Clayton would never allow it within her office."

"You're absolutely right; she wouldn't." Kai grinned and ran his fingers through my hair. "I love it. The color suits you."

I blushed and ducked away from his touch, but I intertwined my fingers with his. We continued to walk along the path that led out of the forest and closer to my house.

Kai glanced around us in awe. "It looks so similar to home."

"It is," I said. "The weather, seasons, and time all work the same. It's really only the people who are different. Many centuries ago, our ancestors lived on Earth, scattered throughout the planet. It's how you continue to have myths of Anubis, centaurs, unicorns, and the like."

"Unicorns are real?" Kai shouted.

"Hush, I'm telling a story." I smiled slyly. "But yes, they are. Anyway, eventually humanity became more wary of the creatures and started to hunt them down. Our numbers were significantly lower than the humans, so many of the creatures fled in terror. The few that managed to survive convened in what is now modern-day Scotland—it was expansive and had a lower population of humans at the time. Still, they knew that one day, the humans would find them and slaughter them all.

"A few who had stronger magic pooled their power together and created a rip in the fabric of space. The Vale is basically a small slice of Earth, but in a pocket realm. It exists next to your universe. Kind of overlaps it. There are a few places where the separation thins, and people will get occasional glances into our world."

"Wait," Kai said, gripping my forearm. "Bigfoot?"

I nodded. "And Nessie, too."

"Oh. My. God." Kai barked an incredulous laugh. "This is insane!"

"Just wait." The smile never dropped from my face. I did love being in the quiet nature of The Vale. The air was more pure, the smells more crisp. Everything seemed to be full of life and more vibrant than on Earth. I had wished my entire life that I could fit in here, but I was too "strange" by Vale standards, and it had made my existence difficult.

We exited the forest into a sleepy neighborhood. It appeared like any other suburb with one and two-story houses spread apart. Lawns with children's toys scattered about, and a few cars here and there. Most of the time, residents of The Vale used bicycles to get around, or their own "horsepower", so to speak. But there were some who didn't have a lower half suitable for either of those options. I never learned how new cars periodically appeared here. Because there were no factories for more modern appliances, but we also had refrigerators, dishwashers, and washing machines, and I didn't know how those were transported either.

Really, life here wasn't so different than on Earth. Kai seemed confused as we walked the block to my house. Adjusting his duffel bag on his shoulder, he glanced at me.

"Uh, where are all the people?"

"Work, school, at the café downtown gossiping. Depends on their age."

"I don't know why, but I assumed nobody worked here."

I laughed loudly. "Of course they do! Otherwise, a town can't run properly. We even have a mayor—Kurjar Thunderhoof. He's a minotaur."

Kai's confusion only increased, and he was about to ask me another question when he was interrupted by a shout from the house we were passing.

"Is that Huckleberry Silverwater-Raad?"

I groaned. My full name was such a mouthful. On Earth, my legal last name was shortened to Silverwater. Please don't tell my dad I dropped his last name. My mom's was simply more fun.

But also, we were only one house away from my own, and I had foolishly thought we would make it without anyone seeing us. I reluctantly slowed and turned to our neighbor Todd, who was heading down his driveway toward us. He was also a cynocephalus, but with the head of a bloodhound. He was dressed in a blue button-down shirt tucked into jeans, and his long ears swayed as he walked. A quick glance to my side showed Kai's eyes about to pop out of his head. With a nudge of my elbow, he cleared his throat and schooled his face, but I could tell he was still woefully unprepared to meet the people of The Vale.

"Hi, Mr. Ambrones," I said, giving him a little wave.

He stopped a few feet away from us and propped his hands on his hips.

"Well, as I live and breathe, it is you, Huckleberry." Drool dripped from his jowls when he spoke. "It's been quite a while since you've been home. How is the human world treating you?"

"Pretty good," I responded, resisting the urge to take a step back and out of the splash zone. "I've been working at my dream job and—"

"Is that Huckleberry?" Another shout from the house, and the wide front door opened again, revealing Todd's husband, Kirios—a centaur. His torso was bare, showcasing an olive skin tone and his long dark hair was kept pulled back in a ponytail. His horse half was a deep brown, and his tail matched his hair color. They were the stereotypical goofy suburban dads, except they didn't have any kids.

He cantered over to meet us and slung his arm over Todd's shoulder.

"Welcome back, young Huck! And, oh," he said, noticing Kai. "Who is this?"

"Todd, Kirios, this is my boyfriend, Kai. He is also human."

Their eyes both went wide. Other than me, there weren't any humans living in The Vale.

"Pleasure to meet you, Kai," Kirios said. "We've been Huck's *neigh*-bors since he was in diapers. We've missed seeing you around! You should visit more often."

"I'll try!" I said, grabbing Kai's hand and starting to walk away. I pointed to our house next door. "We haven't seen my parents yet, so we gotta run."

"Come by for dinner sometime!" Todd shouted after us.

"Will do!" I called over my shoulder. But I would avoid dinner at their house at all costs. Todd couldn't control his slobber around food, and it always ended up on *everyone's* plates. The thought made me throw up in my mouth a little.

Walking up to my childhood home raised such a feeling of nostalgia. I loved this house and my parents. I hadn't wanted to leave them, but I needed to find my own way outside of The Vale.

It was a two-story craftsman-style house, painted in a cheery light yellow with a bright white front door. A covered patio extended the length of the house. A wicker chair, a small table, and a clawfoot bathtub were off to the side. It was one of my mother's favorite spots to relax. The front lawn was grass when I was a child, but as I grew, my mom and I turned it into a flower garden. Now it burst with every color under the sun, and the sweet scent was so familiar I wanted to cry.

It had been almost three years since I'd been here.

At the front door, I paused with my hand on the knob. I couldn't bring myself to turn it. Why was I so nervous? I loved my parents, and they were fully supportive of me. They had known I was gay before *I* even did, so when I "came out" they didn't even bat an eye. My mom just asked me what I wanted for dinner. Relationships were different in The Vale. It wasn't taboo to date between different types of creatures, and gender or expression of sexuality weren't frowned upon. Anyone here could be who they wanted to be. Openly, without fear of repercussions. Except for being human, apparently. Or at least, that was my experience.

I loved that New York City was accepting, but there were still places where it would be safer for me and Kai to pretend we were only friends and nothing more. I wished Earth would be more like The Vale in this instance.

Kai placed a hand on my shoulder. "Are you okay?"

"Yeah," I lied. I really, really hoped this didn't scare Kai away from me. *That* was truly the reason I was nervous. Not because of my parents, but because I loved Kai, and if he left me...I would be devastated. Especially after I put myself out there by bringing him home.

Taking a deep breath, I turned the knob, pushed open the door, and stepped into my house. "Mom? Dad? I'm home."

Seven

THE FRONT DOOR LED into a small hallway with the staircase directly ahead and an open doorway on both sides. Apparently, my mother had painted since I was last home, and the walls were now a shade of lavender, similar to my hair. Well, *our* hair, seeing as I inherited it from her.

I placed my bag down on the ground, and Kai followed suit. There had been no answer to my call, which most likely meant they were in the backyard.

Motioning with my head to follow me, I took the door to the left and walked through a living room cluttered with knick-knacks and well-loved furniture. If Kai hadn't seen my apartment first, I would have cringed at how my parents lived compared to his. But this was how they preferred things. At least, my mom did. My dad would have preferred things to be tidier and organized, but he realized a long time ago it was impossible to keep things that way. And he loved my mom too much to complain.

We wound through the kitchen with an attached breakfast nook. There was a formal dining room off to the side, but it was rarely used. Instead, our meals were eaten at the small table here or on the couch in front of the TV. Finally, we reached the sliding glass door that led to the backyard.

With a grunt, I pushed the door open. It really needed to be greased; it'd only gotten worse in the time I was away. Stepping outside onto a patio with Kai on my heels, I turned and saw my parents at the table underneath an umbrella. My mother was in her preferred water tank, leaning over the side and sipping some tea while conversing with my father, who sat in a normal chair.

Other than her pearlescent tail and fins, I took after my mother. Pale skin, purple hair, and light blue irises. Her siren half was a glimmer of pinks, purples, and greens. I'd always thought it was beautiful and was jealous I couldn't have a tail of my own.

My father could have been the spitting image of Anubis. His head was similar to that of a Doberman with pointed ears, but his fur was sleek and dark black. Shrewd, dark yellow eyes watched my mother with rapt attention. Similar to most other cynocephali, his head and neck were the only parts that resembled a dog—the rest of him was human. His halfway unbuttoned shirt displayed his torso—golden tan skin and well-defined muscles. He wore gold bands on both wrists, and one ear was pierced, sporting a golden hoop earring.

They still hadn't noticed us, too engrossed in their own conversation. I saw Kai standing next to me, his jaw slackened and eyes wide.

"You good?" I whispered.

He nodded slowly. "Your dad is hot," he murmured. "You never told me he was hot. Those muscles..."

I rolled my eyes. "Please don't. People have been drooling over him my entire life."

"Drooling? Who's drooling?" Kai closed his mouth and tried to covertly wipe away a small bit of saliva on his lips. I smiled. Maybe people would think I'd be jealous of my dad in this scenario, but I was secure in my relationship with Kai, and my dad didn't have eyes for anyone other than my mom.

Clearing my throat, I raised my voice and said, "Hi, Mom and Dad."

They both turned to us, my mother beaming and diving underneath the water, only to come up on the edge of the tank near us. Leaning her upper body over the edge, she held her arms out toward me.

"Huckleberry! I'm so glad you made it safely." Her dulcet voice washed over the two of us. It was easy to see how the sirens of old had lured sailors off their ships. Even Kai had been momentarily ensnared, and he blindly ambled forward.

"Mom..." I warned.

"Oops, sorry," she said, her voice taking on a more normal tone. Kai blinked and stopped next to me, looking a little dazed. "I forget how susceptible humans are."

"Kai, I'd like you to meet my parents." I placed my hand on his lower back. "My mom, Itsa, and my dad, Cabbas."

"It's a pleasure to meet you, Kai," my dad rumbled. His deep voice always reminded me of James Earl Jones. When I discovered *The Lion King* as a kid, I'd ask him to recreate the scenes with me like I was Simba. He'd always grumble something about cats and dogs, but eventually would give in to my demands.

"Please," Mom said. "Come sit. We have so much to catch up on."

Kai and I took a seat in the other chairs under the umbrella. The air had a slight nip in it as autumn was fully taking over the land, but the sun continued to shine down brightly. We drank chai while I caught my parents up on the past few years. I would talk to them occasionally, but communication through different realms was difficult. Cell phones didn't work in The Vale. Email was a little more reliable but still spotty. So I had kept things to a minimum.

Plus, my life was fairly mundane. There wasn't much to tell them about. At least, not until I got my job at the Times and started dating Kai. I had told them when we moved in together, because that's when it felt as if things were becoming more serious. Like, they should know about him if we were going to be occupying the same space.

They asked Kai about himself and his family. Ever the personable one, Kai entered conversation with them flawlessly. He never stared or made comments about my parents' appearance. Really, the perfect gentleman. Other humans would not have had the same amount of courtesy.

When the sun began to set, my father smiled—which was really just him baring his teeth—and said he'd go get some dinner together. My mother took to humming a melancholy tune and floating on her back in the water. Her tail reflected the dying light as she moved it up and down.

"How are you feeling?" I asked Kai.

"It's...a lot," he admitted. "But I love your parents. I can see you take after your mother mostly, in looks and personality, but you have your father's tenacity and loyalty."

I blushed, and my face heated more when Kai ran a finger along my cheek. He stared at me in adoration—the way my father looked at my mother. I had always wanted a love similar to theirs, and here it was, sitting right in front of me.

"I do have one question, though," Kai asked haltingly.

"Anything," I said. I wanted Kai to be as comfortable as possible, and I would answer any questions he might have to the best of my ability.

"How exactly..." His sentence trailed off as he stared pointedly at my mother's tail and raised a brow at me. "How did they...you know."

"How did who do what?"

Kai ran a hand down his face. "You're going to actually make me say it. How did your parents—oh God. How do they fuck?"

I grimaced. Any question but that one. *Ew.* The thoughts of my parents... Nope. I refused to let my mind wander there. Before I could say anything, my dad poked his head out the door to tell us dinner was ready.

"Fantastic!" my mother trilled. She hauled herself onto the edge of her water tank and swung herself around. Kai watched it all in fascination. But, oh no, I knew what was coming next. I wasn't fast enough to warn Kai before Itsa Silverwater decided to magic her tail away.

But in doing that, her bare legs and nether regions were exposed. Now only in a bathing suit top, most of her naked body was on display. I clapped a hand over Kai's eyes, and he shouted in surprise, and maybe a bit of pain, too. I wasn't exactly gentle.

"Sorry," I murmured to him. "Mother! Pants!"

"Huckleberry, we raised you not to be so prude about these things," she said while donning a pair of jean shorts she'd left lying nearby. "Really, you should know by now that as creatures we all have—"

"Our differences," I finished for her. "Mom, yes, it's not me I'm worried about. Kai didn't grow up here. He's not accustomed to seeing everyone out in public with their junk hanging out."

I lowered my hand from Kai's eyes, which were twinkling with mischief.

"Junk hanging out, you say? And at least now I have an answer to my earlier question."

"Well, it depends on the creature. Also, gross, don't think about my parents," I said. "You didn't notice Mr. Ambrones earlier?"

Kai's lips tugged into a frown. "He was definitely wearing pants."

"No, not—The *centaur*, Kai. He was not wearing pants. Most centaurs don't, but they have external genitalia like the rest of us."

His mouth dropped open a bit with realization. "I think I was too busy trying to figure out if I was dreaming or not."

I chuckled. "I plan on taking you into town tomorrow. You'll have plenty more chances to gawk at gonads then." My stomach chose that moment to rumble, and I could smell my dad's stir fry. My favorite. I'd missed my dad's home cooking. Kai was a wizard in the kitchen, but there was nothing better than a staple from your youth.

It felt so good to be home. It felt even better to have Kai there with me.

Eight

AFTER A DELICIOUS DINNER, Kai and I grabbed our bags and trudged up the stairs to my childhood bedroom. It hadn't changed much over the years. Glow-in-the-dark stars still adorned my ceiling. My desk was in the corner, with a mess of loose papers containing my early writing. But there were some new boxes shoved over by the closet because my parents needed extra storage, apparently.

I winced a little at my full-size bed. We slept in a king at home, and it would be a tight fit here. Noticing my gaze, Kai came up behind me and wrapped his arms around my waist, nuzzling into my neck.

"It's okay," he said. "It only means I'll be forced to spoon you."

"That doesn't sound too bad," I said, turning in his hold. I drew my hands up his chest and behind his neck.

Kai's mouth dropped open. "Too bad?" he said in mock offense. "I give you all of me—my body and my love—and all I get in return is 'that doesn't sound too bad'?"

I chuckled and kissed him lightly. "Come on, I'm exhausted."

When Kai pouted, I nipped at his lip. The hunger in his eyes made butterflies take flight in my stomach. But my parents' bedroom was right next door, and I'd had enough boyfriends in high school to know (embarrassingly) that they could hear everything through these walls.

We changed into our pajamas—well, I did. Kai only slept in boxers. Not that I was complaining about that. Then we squeezed into the bed. Completely content with Kai at my back and his warm hand underneath my shirt, I began to drift off.

"How are you feeling about today?" Kai asked softly, bringing me back to consciousness.

"Depends," I mumbled. "What are you thinking?"

He was silent for a moment, and I held my breath, wondering what he was going to say.

"It's definitely weird, but not as weird as I thought it was going to be. Your parents are great."

I smiled sleepily and snuggled further back into Kai's chest. A contented sigh left my lips when he pulled me in tighter.

"Then I'm feeling pretty great. Honestly, I'm relieved I told you. It's always felt like this huge weight I've had to carry and for someone else to know is so helpful. I always have to dodge questions about my parents, but for you to have *met* them...It means a lot. Now I can talk about them openly to someone." I yawned sleepily, the warmth of the man behind me easing through my tired body. "Thank you, Kai. For not initially thinking I was crazy and for not being scared off because of where I come from."

His nose ran up the side of my neck, making me shiver. "Love you, Berry."

"I love you, too."

The next day we had a lazy morning in bed, luxuriating in vacation time, and eating my dad's amazing French toast and scrambled eggs.

"Any plans for today?" Mom asked, crossing her long, slender legs. Even when she was in her human form, her skin still had an iridescent hue to it.

"I was going to take Kai downtown," I said around a mouthful of eggs.

"Huckleberry, manners," Dad chastised. I squashed the desire to roll my eyes like a petulant teenager.

"That'll be fun," Mom said. "Oh, be sure you take him to Derry's."

"I don't know…"

"What is Derry's?" Kai asked, glancing between the two of us.

"It's an ice cream shop," I said. And I saw Kai opening his mouth to tell me how much he loved ice cream, so I added, "The owner is a kudan who uses her own milk to make it."

His jaw paused mid-bite, and he scrunched up his nose.

"Yeah, I'll probably pass on that one. Thank you for the suggestion, though, Itsa."

My mom smiled pleasantly at him. "Anytime, dear."

There was another ice cream place I could take him to instead. One that used the kind of milk we were accustomed to. Besides, I'd never liked the flavor of Derry's. I hated being dragged there as a kid because it was Mom's favorite dessert shop, and once I learned exactly *how* it was being made...never again. I shuddered.

Shoveling the last few bites into my mouth, I grabbed Kai's hand and pulled him through the house.

"We'll see you later!" I called out to my parents.

"Be safe!" my dad shouted back.

"Don't do anything I wouldn't do!" my mom said.

I laughed and peered at Kai. "That's not saying much. My mom has been known to get a little crazy."

"Really," he drawled, grinning. "I never would have guessed."

Walking around to the garage, I pulled the door open. Manually, because my parents had never thought to upgrade to an automatic one that only required the push of a button. Inside were two beach cruisers—one black and one pink. They were my parents', but they had said we could borrow them for the day. Kai took the black one because he was the taller of the two of us, and we were off.

Cool wind blew back my hair, and it felt so good to be able to let the lavender show. I hated constantly dyeing it to conform with the rest of the humans. And yes, I knew people paid lots of money to achieve this color in the salon, but Ms. Clayton would take one look at it and send me to clean out my desk. Fun wasn't necessarily allowed in my office, but that didn't stop it from being my dream job. I only needed to make a name for myself, and then I could find somewhere less uptight.

Kai wore an easy smile as we rode our bikes through the neighborhood, and I led us toward downtown. Houses and autumn-colored trees lined the streets, with some evergreens scattered around, adding a sense of vitality. It was late enough in the day that most people had already gone to work or school, and we were alone on the streets. An occasional car would pass by, and I'd lift my hand in a silent hello. Either nobody recognized me, or nobody cared enough to stop. That was the way I preferred things, honestly. I loathed unnecessary public interactions.

We reached the city center, and I directed Kai to a bike rack next to the general store. Downtown was blocked to car and bike traffic. It was strictly pedestrian only. A circular area had wall to wall stores and restaurants, and in the center stood a wide gazebo. Many weddings were held here, and there were a series of concerts throughout most of the year where the band used the gazebo as a stage.

"Man, you weren't kidding when you compared it to Stars Hollow," Kai said, turning in a circle with his hands on his hips. He beamed at me. "It's adorable."

"I want to show you my favorite shop," I said, interlacing our fingers. Two doors down from us, there was a candy store. I'd dated the owner's son in high school and had gained several pounds from all the free candy. Worth it, though. Their homemade fudge was to die for.

A little bell rang overhead as we entered the space. Chocolatey aromas flooded my nostrils, and I took a deep inhale. There were other notes of almond, vanilla, and peppermint. I could live in this store. Eat my own weight's worth of candy every day and still never tire of it.

"Huck?"

Oh no. I forced a smile onto my face and turned toward the side of the store. Standing behind the counter was my ex from high school. He was a centaur with golden hair and a sleek palomino coat on his horse half to match. If he were on Earth, he'd be described as a "gym bro". His pectorals and abs were all on display and, if possible, he'd only gotten hotter since we broke up. That just was not fair.

"Hey, Thad," I said with a little wave. When it seemed as though the centaur was going to come around the counter and into the main area of the store, I leaned into Kai's ear. "Abort. Abort. We need to leave *now*."

"Huh? Why? But I want chocolate." He was almost whining like a toddler. And yes, I understood. I also wanted chocolate.

"That's my ex," I hissed, and tried to ease back out the door, but it was too late.

Big arms wrapped around my center in a bruising hug, lifting me off the ground. On the verge of passing out from a lack of oxygen, Thad finally placed me back on my feet. I gasped as I regained my breath, resting my hands on my knees. Wheezing, I waved between Thad and Kai.

"Kai, this is Thadenos. Thad, Kai."

"Woah, another human," Thad said. "It's nice to meet you." Instead of a bone-crushing hug, Kai received a simple handshake.

"You too," Kai said, smirking slyly. "So you two used to date?"

"Back in high school, yeah," said Thad. He ruffled my hair, and I frowned.

I cleared my throat. "You're still working in the shop?"

"Nah," he said, gazing around the room with pride. "My parents retired last year. It's all mine now."

"Oh, that's really great. I'm happy you're doing well." I genuinely was. Thad was a super nice guy. We were simply too different. When we'd broken up, it had been an amicable split, and I cared about his happiness.

"And you?" he asked, suddenly looking concerned. "You're okay over in the human realm? I worry about you."

Aww. "I'm fine," I reassured him. "I've got Kai."

Not that I was expecting jealousy from Thad, but the beaming smile he directed at Kai took me by surprise.

"Good. That's good. I'm happy for you, Huck."

And he seemed to be telling the truth. Still, as friendly as things were between us, this was beginning to turn awkward for me.

Gesturing over my shoulder toward the door, I said, "We've got to get going. I was giving Kai a tour of the town."

"Wait for just a second," Thad said, and turned to go to the back of the store. I could tell when Kai saw it because his eyes bugged out and his jaw opened slightly. I let him gawk, and only cleared my throat when Thad came back, a bag in his hand.

"Here you go," he said, holding the bag out to me. "Fudge on the house. I remember how much you like it."

"Thank you, Thad. That's really kind of you."

As I hustled Kai out of the store, practically shoving him outside, he glanced over our shoulders.

"It was nice to meet you, Thad!" Kai said.

"You too! Come back anytime. I'll hook you up!"

Kai rounded on me the second the door shut behind us, throwing his hands up in the air.

"Thad is hung like a literal horse and you *broke up with him*?" he whisper-yelled at me.

I rubbed the back of my neck. "If you can believe it, I was the top in that relationship."

Shock rippled across Kai's face, and he glanced at me then peered through the window. Thad was standing behind the counter and waved at us. I waved back.

"How...?"

"You don't want to know."

"I kind of do," Kai protested.

"I promise you. You don't."

"I promise *you*. I *do*."

Sighing dramatically, I dropped my head back and let the sun shine down on my face.

"Let's just say it involved a stepladder and leave it at that."

Nine

FOR LUNCH, I TOOK Kai to a 1950s-style diner with the greasiest food imaginable. Just like on Earth, the wait staff were on roller skates, except it was run by a family of cuca. They were creatures originally from Brazil with the head of an alligator and the body of a human. The couple who owned the business had a veritable gaggle of children, and they were all roped into helping. The despondent teenager at the register looked Kai up and down, then rolled her eyes and showed us to a table.

We creature-watched as we ate our sinfully delicious, artery-clogging burgers. I would point out different species to Kai and if I knew some of their background, I'd tell him that too. It was a pleasant lunch, even if the diner was noisy as hell.

After we ate, I took him to the other side of town, where a small creek ran through. We sat on the bank, keeping out of the frigid water, and skipped stones. At the moment, there was nobody else there, and I took the time to revel in being in my hometown with the man I loved.

"Lunch was fun," Kai said. "I don't think I've ever heard you talk so much at one time."

Oh. "Sorry, I just—"

"It's not a bad thing, Berry," he said, threading his fingers into mine. "I love the sound of your voice. I love watching you when you're excited about something. Honestly, I could listen to you talk forever."

"Forever?"

Kai nodded, and leaning into my shoulder, he pressed a kiss onto my cheek. How he still managed to make me blush after six months of dating was beyond me.

"I love you," I murmured, staring into his warm brown eyes. The words weren't enough. They'd never be enough to convey how I felt about Kai, but I hoped he could see the depths of my affection every time I looked at him.

"I love you too, Berry." This time, he kissed me on the lips. His one hand stayed wrapped in mine, and his other came up to brush his thumb along my jaw. When his hand reached the back of my head, he gripped my hair and pulled me tighter to him, deepening our kiss. I moaned into his mouth.

Before I could climb into his lap, a small cough sounded near us, and I remembered we were in public. Turning to the creek, I saw a lamia—a woman with a snake's body—staring daggers at us.

"Sorry," I said with a wince.

With a little *hmph* sound, she slithered down the creek.

"Maybe not the best location for a makeout session," Kai chuckled. I grinned at him sheepishly and tried to ignore how tight my pants were.

Clearing my throat, I said, "I promised you ice cream. Let me take you to The Corner Creamery. They have the best gelato I've ever tasted."

"None of this cool down milk, though, right?"

I barked a laugh. "It's kudan! And, no, just good ole regular cow's milk."

The visible relief on Kai's face made me chuckle. Then he grabbed my hand and darted off back toward the main square. The man really did enjoy his ice cream.

We spent the rest of the afternoon milling around town and popping into various shops. Everyone greeted us warmly and welcomed me back. It was a stark contrast to how they'd treated me as a kid. Mr. Granuk—a minotaur who, ironically enough, owned a fine china store—even gave me a hug. This was from someone who shooed me out of his establishment when I was twelve years old because it was no place for "human rats." I had been shopping for a present for my mom's birthday. After that, I avoided him at all costs.

Sunset caught us sitting on a brick wall on the outskirts of the main square. The gazebo was painted in orange and pink light as a band set up within the quaint space. Creatures of all kinds milled about, gathering to hear the music. They held these concerts once a week while the weather was pleasant. When winter took over, they would stop, then start up again in the spring. There weren't many bands in The Vale—it can be hard to play certain instruments when you don't have the correct anatomy—and that night was a teenage, garage punk band. The kids bantered with each other as they set up amps and speakers, and I smiled at their antics.

Kai reached over and intertwined his fingers with mine, and I rested my head on his shoulder.

"What kind of creature is that?" Kai asked, nodding toward a man with short horns and the lower body of a goat.

"A satyr. You know, like Mr. Tumnus."

"Who?"

I pulled my head back and stared at Kai incredulously.

"You've never read *The Lion, The Witch, and The Wardrobe*?"

Kai frowned at me. "No. Isn't that the one with the Jesus lion?"

I almost choked. "You haven't even seen the movie?"

He laughed as he shook his head. "Sorry, Berry. It wasn't really my scene. I'm not a big reader, and the movies I used to watch were more of the action variety."

Before my brain could process this blasphemy, Kai pointed at a creature with the body of a man, but the head of a horse.

"Is that some kind of reverse centaur?" he asked.

"Technically, yes," I said. "They're called ipotane."

This continued for a few minutes. Kai asked me about some of the more obscure creatures. Humans obviously knew about them and myths, but not all of them had crossed into modern-day pop culture. Fantasy movies and books depicted only a small percentage of the creatures actually in existence.

My parents eventually arrived and sat on the wall with us. My mother sat next to Kai and my father next to me. She wore her human legs as she usually did while out in the town. It was easier for her to transport herself on dry land that way. However, she could only maintain the form for a couple of hours at a time, so they wouldn't be staying for the entire concert.

Every year while I still lived at home, we would go to the coast for a vacation. My father and I would stay in a small beach house while my mother swam in the warm sea. Typically, her family would meet us there and we'd have a fun week together, splashing in the waves. Although my cousins never understood why I couldn't breathe underwater, and they regarded me strangely when I couldn't dive lower than ten feet.

Itsa loved it, though, and I loved seeing my mother happy. If she didn't get time in the sea, she would turn despondent. I hoped she and my dad continued to go.

Once the music began, people danced around the square. Kai and I hopped off the wall and tried to join them. Glances were thrown our way. Nobody was saying anything, but I could feel the eyes on me.

Suddenly, I was transported back to when I was a child and everybody stared at me like I was something "other." Cold sweat broke out on my brow and I backed away toward the wall. Kai furrowed his brow.

"What's wrong?" he asked.

I couldn't answer him. My breathing rate increased. My heart pounded in my chest. This was why I hadn't been home in so long. The stares and judgment. It was too much.

"I want to go home," I whimpered.

"Okay," Kai said reassuringly. "We can go."

Trying to focus on my breathing, I barely noticed as Kai told my parents we were leaving. My mother looked at me with concern.

"Are you okay, Huckleberry?"

"Fine," I managed to gasp out. Itsa frowned but didn't push. My parents didn't know about all the trouble I'd been given as a child. I hadn't wanted to burden them with it. One time, I had told my dad about something—I couldn't even remember what it was now–but he stormed out of the house. After he came back, saying he'd fixed the problem, it had only made it worse. So, I stopped mentioning anything.

"Come on," Kai murmured directly in my ear.

Numbly, I followed his lead as he guided me back to my parents' house.

Ten

"OKAY, BERRY, TELL ME what's going on," Kai said as soon as the front door to the house closed behind us. My parents had stayed to watch more of the concert, but they'd be home soon.

"Nothing. It's fine," I said, darting for the kitchen. Filling a glass with ice-cold water, I chugged it and finally began to feel some semblance of calm. Kai followed me.

"That's bullshit, and we both know it," he said.

"I'm okay, Kai. Just...had a little panic attack is all." I couldn't look at him, instead staring very intently at a drop of water running down the outside of my cup. Kai shuffled up behind me and brushed his fingers gently down the back of my neck. I shivered.

"Do you want to talk about it?" Kai murmured.

I shook my head. "Not really."

"You know I'm here for you, right?"

Of course, I knew that. I nodded. Kai's fingers trailed down my spine reassuringly, and he placed a light kiss behind my ear, forcing a giggle out of me at the tickling sensation.

"I'm going to take a shower," Kai said softly, still so close. The heat of his body radiated into my own. "Join me?"

Yes, this was exactly the distraction I needed. Grabbing Kai's hand, I hauled him up the stairs. We lovingly stripped each other's clothes off as the water heated and the room filled with steam. Kisses and touches were exchanged, and inside the shower Kai reminded me how much love he had for me.

Afterwards, we were lying in bed, and Kai snored lightly. I couldn't sleep. Glow-in-the-dark stars clung stubbornly to my ceiling, and I traced the patterns and constellations I'd tried to create when I was seven.

Nobody had said anything to either of us tonight, but I could feel the weight of their judgment all the same. Two humans didn't belong in The Vale. It didn't matter that my parents were creatures, and I'd simply been some sort of genetic fluke. Memories and fear ran deep, and the creatures were wary of humans.

So instead of overcoming their generational trauma, they tore me down.

These creatures *knew* me. They knew I'd never hurt anyone. That I loved my community. At least, I had until I realized how cruel everyone could be. How disingenuous they all were. They'd say what a handsome boy I was to my parents' faces, then spit on the ground in front of my feet when I was alone. The second I turned eighteen, I begged my parents to let me move to the human lands. To be with people who looked like me. My mother had cried, but they both agreed to let me leave and they retrieved a portal for me the next day.

It was great to see my parents and the people who were decent to me—Thad, for example. But two weeks was a long time. I felt the longer I stayed, the more looks I would get. Next, the whispers would start. If we visited in the future, it would need to be for shorter periods of time. I didn't think my anxiety could handle much more.

The next morning, I took Kai to a few places we hadn't visited yet. The Vale had no shortage of cute and cozy little nooks—bookstores, coffee shops, various knick-knacks. Creatures loved their knick-knacks.

We were walking out of a café with lattes in hand when someone bumped into Kai's shoulder in the doorway. He opened his mouth to apologize, then froze. His eyes went wide as he stared at the creature.

I could understand why. In front of us stood a gigantic moth with large, multifaceted red eyes, antennae that scraped the doorjamb, and fluttering wing…all wrapped up in a red flannel shirt and jeans.

He scowled at Kai (well, as much as a moth could scowl), and said, "It's rude to stare." His voice had a muffled, buzzing quality to it. Finally, he noticed me standing there and nodded.

"Huck," the moth said. "Good to see you."

A vibrating sound came from him as he shoved past us into the building. I turned to stare at him.

"In *public*, Dave?" I asked him, but he never acknowledged me. "And he called *us* rude." I grabbed Kai's elbow and guided him onto the sidewalk. He was visibly shaken and still wide-eyed.

"Was that fucking *Mothman*?" he asked in a frenzied whisper.

"His name is Dave. I went to high school with him."

"But he's a moth."

"He is," I agreed.

Kai ran a hand down his face and began to calm. "What did you mean by 'in public'?"

Pink tinged my cheeks as I blushed. "Oh, well, there's this thing moths can do—actual moths in the human lands do this too, by the way." Oh no, I was rambling. "But, uh, he can…"

"Can what?" Kai asked, his shock turning to amusement at my obvious discomfort.

"He can kind of vibrate his genitals."

He gaped at me. "And you know this *how*?"

I rubbed the back of my neck. "We maybe had a thing during senior year?"

Kai's jaw dropped further.

"It was only for one night!" I hastened to add. "Dave liked to sleep around a lot. I'm pretty sure everyone our age has fucked him at least once. And when I heard about the vibrating thing, I was curious."

Kai took a long sip of his coffee, staring out into space. "Man, this place really keeps you on your toes, huh?"

I chuckled, relieved. "You get used to it."

Then he turned that brilliant smile that I loved toward me and took my hand, intertwining our fingers.

"I don't know that I'd ever get used to it, Berry. But it sure is fun. I think I like it here."

The words should have warmed my heart. Kai was talking about my hometown. The place I had grown up and spent all my formative years. But the twinkle in his eye as he gazed upon the quaint town square only filled me with dread.

Eleven

ABOUT HALFWAY THROUGH OUR trip, I awoke one morning to find Kai's side of the bed empty and cold. Rubbing my eyes, I plodded downstairs in my pajamas. The sound of roaring laughter emanated from the kitchen, waking me up slightly. Kai and my parents were sitting around the table—Itsa floated in one of her water tanks—with coffee in front of them. Tears leaked down my mother's face as she listened to Kai. He was always so animated when he told stories, waving his hands about, making faces, and imitating the voices of the other people involved.

I leaned against the doorframe and watched for a moment. Normally the stoic one, even my dad was cracking up. Cabbas had a loud bark for a laugh, and he was clutching his stomach. I'd never seen him like this. He wasn't shedding tears but then again, I'd never actually seen my father cry. I wasn't even sure if he was physically capable.

The sight warmed my soul. It was amazing to see Kai and my parents getting along so well together. I had never brought anyone home before—not in the traditional sense, anyway. Thad had been my most serious relationship, and I hadn't ever properly introduced him to my parents. They had known about him, of course, and the town was so small that everybody knew who was dating whom. But I'd never brought him home for dinner. Or to family functions. Anyway, most of the time we were at his house because he couldn't fit up the staircase to get to my bedroom.

Itsa finally noticed me standing there. "Huckleberry, dear, come join us. Kai was just telling us—" She broke off into a fit of giggles.

My dad tried to compose himself and opened his mouth to say something, but all that came out was another bark of laughter. I smiled and sat at the table.

Raising a brow at Kai, I asked, "What were you talking about?"

He smirked. "Oh, I was only regaling them with the story of our first date when you got so drunk on sake that I practically had to carry you home."

Halfheartedly, I scowled at him. "It's not funny. I was extremely hungover the next day. And that wasn't our first date."

"Maybe not officially, no," Kai said, beaming at me. "But it was when I realized I wanted to see you more."

My heart skipped a beat.

"That was the first day we met," I reminded him.

"I know." His eyes softened as he gazed at me, and a vast wave of love for this man suffused my entire body. How I'd ever gotten so lucky was beyond me.

"I can honestly say you're the best person I've ever literally run into," I said.

"Happens often, does it?"

"Oh yes," Itsa chimed in. She smiled broadly, glancing between the two of us. "Huckleberry is quite clumsy."

I rolled my eyes. "Thank you for that, Mother."

"It's true, though," my dad grumbled. Could my eyes roll back further into my head?

Kai placed his hand on my thigh, giving me that look again, like I was his entire world. My lungs nearly stopped functioning.

"I'm thankful for it, all the same. Otherwise I might not have met you and I'd be missing out on all of this."

Clearing her throat, my mom leaned forward and rested her elbows on the edge of her tank. "It's a gorgeous day outside. Dear, why don't you show Kai the walking path through the forest?"

She was darting pointed glances between me and Kai, then shifted her gaze to my father and her eyes softened. My dad stared back at her and...Oh, dear God. They wanted the house to themselves. I glanced at Kai in horror, and thankfully he read the situation and nudged me out of the kitchen. We raced upstairs, dressed in record time, and were out of the house before my parents had made it to their bedroom.

Once we were safely in the forest, far enough away from the house that we wouldn't be able to hear anything, we broke down giggling. Our mirth ebbed and, for me, morphed into a quiet awe as I appreciated my surroundings.

The trees had all changed color, and the canopy was painted gold, maroon, and various shades of orange. Leaves fluttered to the ground occasionally, and they crunched as we walked over them. Birds sang in the treetops and flitted between the branches. The slight nip in the air filled my lungs with clean oxygen—something I'd definitely been missing in New York City. Fall was my favorite season, and this was why. There is a peaceful quality to the world. Like the earth was gently falling asleep...yawning deeply before descending into hibernation. It was beautiful.

Hand in hand, Kai and I meandered slowly down the wooden boardwalk. There was a group of volunteers who kept the way clear—preserving the natural wonder while simultaneously clearing it of poison ivy.

I exhaled and let my stress wash away. Although I loved seeing my parents, being around everyone else in town was simply...a lot. I was walking on eggshells. They had all been nice to us so far, but I was waiting for the other shoe to drop. My anxiety had been spiking like crazy.

And though I loved seeing Kai light up as I showed him around The Vale, I couldn't wait to get home to our quiet apartment.

From a bend up around the corner, giggles bounced around the trees, shattering the peaceful trance I had found myself in. Kai and I slowed and moved to the side, intending to let the group of creatures pass us by.

Three harpies came into view. Gorgeous young women with the bodies of birds. Well, mostly. Their torsos, arms, and legs were humanoid, but their feet were those of an eagle, tipped with fierce talons, and they had massive wings attached to their backs. All three had long, wavy blonde hair of varying shades, and they wore autumnal clothing in the style of humans. I wouldn't have been surprised to find pumpkin spice lattes in their hands. I recognized all of them from high school; they'd been two grades above me.

They were talking and laughing, completely oblivious of our presence on the path. Until the one in the middle—I could not remember any of their names for the life of me—glanced up. She saw me and started, but when she looked at Kai, she completely stopped in her tracks. Her mouth fell open, and her friends gazed at her with concern.

"Kai?" she said, shock ringing through her voice.

I glanced up at Kai, confused, and saw him staring back at her. His jaw had also become unhinged.

"Melissa?" he said incredulously.

"What are you doing here?" she asked, her voice rising an octave.

"Me? You're..." He gestured toward her. "You're a–a—" Kai stumbled on his words.

"Harpy," I murmured.

"A *harpy*?" he finished.

It was my turn to frown and glance between the two. Luckily, Melissa's friends seemed to be as lost as I was.

"You...know each other?" I asked.

"We dated in college," Kai replied, sounding dazed.

Huh? He couldn't possibly mean *this* Melissa. Maybe it was someone who looked similar? Because Melissa had wings. And scaled feet with talons. Also, I thought I was the only one who had left The Vale for an extended period. I knew others would go occasionally for supplies, but for college? That was something else altogether.

Kai had to be mistaken.

"Huh?" I said out loud.

"We dated in college," Melissa confirmed.

"But you didn't look like...this," Kai said, vaguely gesturing at her wings and feet.

Melissa rolled her eyes. "Duh. Can't exactly walk around in the human lands like this. I was using a glamour."

"Are you telling me you went to college in the human lands?" I asked her.

Crossing her arms across her (ample) chest, Melissa glared at me. Her two friends did the same.

"What, you think you're the only one special enough to go, *Huckleberry*?" She scoffed, and I held back a wince. "What are you even doing back here anyway?"

This. This is exactly why I had left in the first place. To escape the "mean girl" attitude that so many used against me. I was ready to turn around and walk back home, but Kai's warm hand slipped into my own. Tugging me into his side, he glared right back at Melissa.

"He brought me to meet his parents," Kai told her. Nuzzling into my ear, he murmured, "Don't worry about her. She's always been a jerk."

A nervous giggle escaped me. He wasn't wrong. I turned my head slightly so that only he could hear me.

"So why were you dating her?"

"Because I was an eighteen-year-old boy away from home for the first time, and all I could see was a set of great tits. Once I realized who she really was, I broke things off."

Melissa and her cronies watched our exchange with pursed lips. A set of claws tapped on the boardwalk impatiently.

"You're dating *him*?" she asked with a sneer.

"Of course I am," Kai answered. "Because he's kind-hearted, selfless, brilliant..."

He peered down at me, smiling, and my heart warmed at his words. The amount of love I had for him was—

Kai interrupted my thoughts. "And he's got a great dick."

I choked, and Melissa gaped at us. Kai tugged me forward and shoved past the three harpies. They could only stare at us as we walked away. I wanted to turn my head to see if they were still watching us, but Kai twitched against my hand.

"Don't," he said lowly. "Showing them our backs will hurt them more. Don't ever let a bully see they're affecting you."

It was sage advice and something I would need to remember for the future. I'd always curled in on myself whenever I was bullied—never stood up for myself, never walked away with my head held high. They only teased me more for it.

Jealousy kindled in my gut a few minutes later after we were far enough away from Melissa.

"Dated her simply because of boobs, huh?" I said, trying to keep my voice light and sarcastic, but some of my insecurity leaked through. Kai glanced at me with a brow raised.

"Don't give me any of that jealous bullshit, Berry. In the past week, I've met two of your exes. One of which is literally hung like a horse and the other has vibrating genitals. So, yes, I dated her because of boobs."

My face flushed. "Sorry," I murmured.

Kai playfully jostled my shoulder. "You can make it up to me later."

Now my stomach flipped, and my face turned a deeper shade of red. "Oh, really?"

"Yeah," Kai said, his voice dropping dangerously low. His nose ran up the shell of my ear, making me shiver. "You can buy me ice cream."

Laughing at the disappointment that must have been plastered over my face, Kai kissed my cheek, then turned his face toward the sky. He was beautiful like this. His dark hair shone in the sunlight; his smile was brighter than I'd ever seen it.

Kai turned to me, a mischievous glint in his eye. "Race you!" he called and took off running down the boardwalk.

Chuckling, I shook my head and shoved my hands in my pockets. I followed him at a leisurely pace, giving me time to think. If Melissa had gone to college on Earth, who else had gone over from The Vale without my knowledge?

Twelve

WE'D SPENT THE PAST week exploring more of the town and taking some small day trips. There was a canyon lake nearby that was beautiful, and a separate grove of trees, which was home to a large colony of fairies. They could be hostile, but as long as you brought them some kind of gift, they let you walk about freely. The small city they'd built within the trees was always a marvel to see, and the sun glinting off their iridescent wings was gorgeous.

The Vale was more than just the town. An entire world existed beyond the city boundaries—waterfalls, oceans, plains, and forests. This was simply where all the human-esque creatures settled. The town had modern technology (except for internet and cell service), but I'd heard rumors of other smaller settlements that continued to live as if it were the Middle Ages.

Out in the wilds, non-humanoid creatures roamed freely. Things like manticores, pegasus, kelpies, griffins, and more. Some people thought there were dragons or wyverns hiding somewhere, but there were no known sightings of them.

When I was explaining all of this to Kai, his face lit up more and more with each new tidbit of information. Finally, he asked me very excitedly if we could go on a safari and was crestfallen when I told him one didn't exist.

For the rest of the day, he tried to pitch me with a new business venture. When I mentioned how dangerous it would be—a manticore is basically a pissed off lion that can fly and is also venomous—he said we could simply buy armored cars. He was willing to front the entire thing with his own money, and I finally had to tell him I'd think about it so he would drop the subject.

One, I didn't think it was actually something that people would want. And two, that meant spending more time in The Vale, which I absolutely did not want to do.

Saturday afternoon rolled around again, and we were back in the town square, sitting on the brick wall and waiting for the concert to start. Creatures of all kinds sat on blankets and camp chairs scattered around the gazebo. Sirens could be seen either in inflatable pools or in their human form. Centaurs folded their legs underneath them to relax on the ground. Even the reclusive cyclops, Gorix, sat on the edge of the crowd. I'd seen him only maybe three times in my entire life.

The band began to play. Tonight, it was a tree nymph. Her skin was a deep brown and cracked, similar to bark, and her leafy hair hung from her head like a willow tree. Angelic music flowed from her mouth in a slow melody. Creatures swayed where they sat, and some couples stood to dance.

"Dance with me." Kai's soft murmur tickled my ear. I turned to see him staring at me reverently, bowed at the waist slightly, hand outstretched.

I eased my hand into his without hesitation, and we hopped off the wall. Kai pulled me close to him, and we rocked back and forth in time with the song. There were no formal steps; he led me, and I followed. I would always follow him.

Brilliant white teeth flashed at me. "Do you remember the first time we danced?"

I frowned. "You mean at the club?"

"Yes," Kai said, his smile growing.

"The club called DIX? Where you made me take a *blowjob* shot?"

Kai chuckled. "That's the one."

"That was a decidedly different type of dancing."

"True. But it was also our first kiss."

My heart rate kicked up. I remembered it well. It was also the first night we spent together, and I had already known that I was falling for Kai.

"I plan on giving you plenty more, Berry," Kai whispered. I tucked my head against his chest. He pulled me slightly closer, and his sigh ruffled my hair. "This is nice, though. Everything here is. Thank you for bringing me to your home, especially because I know it hasn't been super easy for you."

I could only tighten my arms around his middle. Listening to Kai talk was one of my favorite pastimes, and if I stayed quiet, he would continue to ramble. His deep voice reverberated through his chest, and I reveled in the sound of it and the warmth radiating off his body.

"Huckleberry..." Kai hedged.

Oh no. He never called me by my full name. It was always only Huck or Berry. *Never* the whole thing. Was he going to break up with me? *Calm down, Huck. He just said he wants to give you more kisses.* Okay, so maybe not that. But it couldn't be anything good.

"What would you think about moving here?" he finally asked.

My entire body stiffened. Easing back from Kai, our feet slowed until we stopped, and I could only gape at him. He grimaced, but didn't remove his arms from around me.

"I realize you've had some poor experiences here in the past, but I really think everyone has—"

"I can't," I whispered, horrified. My stomach tied itself in knots, and I suddenly had the urge to vomit.

"Berry... Is it something we can talk through? It could be a good move for us."

I shook my head. Without realizing it, I'd dropped my embrace and was taking several steps away from Kai. The hurt on his face was almost more than I could bear. But the familiar feeling of a panic attack started in my chest. My lungs felt constricted. My face and hands were tingling. I couldn't talk about this. Not right now. Not here.

Continuing to walk away, I shook my head again. "I can't." I choked on a sob.

"Huck, please," Kai pleaded, reaching out to me.

"I'm sorry."

Before the tears could flow, I turned and sprinted back to my house. Flinging myself on top of my bed, I sobbed into my pillow. Something all too reminiscent of my days back in high school.

Soft footfalls on my bedroom floor pulled me out of my stupor. My bed dipped, and Kai's familiar scent wrapped around me. Normally, it was comforting. Now, it meant I'd need to have a conversation I greatly wished to avoid.

His hand landed gently on my back and rubbed soothing circles. I took a deep breath and exhaled with a shudder.

"Huck," Kai murmured. "I never wanted to hurt you, and I'm sorry I sent you into this state. But please can we at least discuss it?"

Rolling onto my side, dislodging Kai's hand in the process, I wiped at my tear-streaked face.

"Kai, I need you to understand," I said. "The things people put me through here... They were *horrible* to me. They would spit at my feet. Compliment me to my parents, then glare at me once their backs were turned. They'd call me a freak, and other names I'd rather not repeat. I was ostracized by almost everyone here. A few befriended me, of course. But in high school, I threw myself into sex, trying to have it as much as possible because it let me forget. For a few minutes, it would let me forget. But even with that, many of my partners only slept with me because I was 'exotic'. As soon as we finished, they would sneer at me and kick me out. I left The Vale as soon as I could."

Tears threatened again as I spoke, but I pushed them back. I was tired of crying over these people.

"You think I don't understand where you're coming from?" Kai asked. "I'm second generation Japanese-American. My parents had money, so I went to a private school where everyone was mostly white. There were a few other non-Caucasian kids, but I mostly felt extremely alone. I was also ostracized, made fun of, called names. Kids would push me down and steal my lunch. They'd tear apart my homework and lie about it when I told the teacher. High school was not a great time for me, either. And similarly to you, I turned to something that could make me forget. But for me, it was alcohol. By my junior year, I was drinking every day after school. My parents actually sent me to a rehab center once they found out, and I was there for two weeks. My God, once the other kids learned that's where I was, it became even worse."

"I'm so sorry," I whispered.

"Once I went to college, it all changed. There was so much more diversity, and I was included in things because people actually liked me for *me*. They saw more than the color of my skin or the shape of my eyes. I'm sure you felt the same when you came to the human lands and finally could be surrounded by people who looked like you."

I nodded.

"My point, Huck," Kai continued, "is that I completely understand your childhood experiences, because I lived them as well. Same story, different font. I want you to understand I would never willingly put you in a situation where I thought you would be hurt—physically or emotionally."

"I know that," I murmured, taking his hand and squeezing it.

"That being said, the creatures here seem to have changed. They're treating you like they are anyone else."

"Melissa..."

Kai slashed his hand through the air. "Melissa is a bitch to everyone. It's not just you, trust me."

My breath hitched. "But they all are giving me these *looks*."

"Berry," Kai said, smoothing my hair off my face. "I think they're only surprised to see you back. You've been gone for so long, and you told me before that when you'd visit, you would only stay here. They haven't seen you in forever, and your sudden appearance has them curious. But they're not being mean or malicious."

Could he be right about that? I frowned and retreated inside myself. Could they all have actually changed and now don't care that I'm human?

No. People weren't capable of change like that. I'd seen racist humans on Earth behave the same way, and they never learned, no matter who talked to them.

"I think—" Kai started, but I interrupted him.

"I don't want to talk about it anymore."

Rolling over to the wall, I turned my back to Kai. He sighed and climbed into the bed behind me, facing away. It felt so wrong. Typically, we slept as intertwined as possible. This gap was not normal for us, and the small space between our bodies was cold. Neither of us said anything else, and I eventually drifted to sleep.

The next morning, I awoke, and the spot next to me was vacant and cold. Kai had been gone for a while then. Yawning, I propped myself up and noticed a note on my nightstand. In a panic, I snatched it up and ran my eyes across the page. I exhaled in relief when it only said that Kai was going for a walk.

I stretched my arms overhead as I plodded downstairs. I'd let Kai go for a walk to clear his head while I ate breakfast. If he didn't make it back soon, I'd go searching for him. I would have to bring my dad to sniff him out, though.

Itsa sat in one of her tubs at the breakfast nook, nursing a cup of coffee. I poured myself a mug and added milk and sugar until it was a light brown color. Easing into a chair next to my mother, we sat in silence for several minutes.

Her melodic voice eventually broke the quiet. "I spoke with Kai this morning."

"Oh?" I said, trying to keep my tone neutral. But inside, my heart beat faster and butterflies erupted in my stomach.

"Don't play coy with me, Huckleberry," she chided, raising her brow over the rim of her cup. "You know the walls are thin and we could hear your argument last night."

I opened my mouth to reply, but my mom cut me off.

"Listen, while I would absolutely love to have you move back home, you need to do what's right for you."

"I just..." I paused. "When I was a kid... Well, mostly in high school, but—" This was hard. I'd never spoken to my parents about the way people treated me. I had never wanted to bring them down with me.

"Honey," she said. Her warm—yet slightly wet—hand covered my own. "We know."

Frowning, I studied her face, currently open and serious, instead of her normal flighty personality. I took in her lavender-colored hair, the exact shade as mine. Her blue gaze mirrored my own and tears welled in her eyes.

"You know?" I asked, confused.

"About how the people of The Vale treated you. You might think we had no idea, but there were subtle tells. Or someone didn't realize we could still see or hear them when they did something rude. Your father, more than once, returned to chastise the adults or speak with the childrens' parents."

I gaped at her. "*Chastise?*"

Itsa nodded. "Sometimes with words. Sometimes with fists."

"No," I said in horror. "That's exactly what I *didn't* want him to do. I thought it would only make things worse for me."

"That's what I told him as well, but you know Cabbas. He always believes people should automatically do the right thing, and when they don't, he wants to show them the error of their ways. Plus, you're his son, Huckleberry. He would do anything to protect you."

Gazing into my coffee, I thought back on my childhood and how different it was compared to now, being in The Vale as an adult. I cringed at how I had treated Kai the night before. It had been unfair of me, and he didn't deserve that.

"What do I do?" I finally asked, looking back up at my mother, who had been sitting in silence, letting me process everything. My mom had always been a strong empath. I don't know why I ever thought I could hide things from her.

"Well, that's not really something I can decide for you. You need to figure out what is most important to you. Is that your job and New York City? Or is it Kai? I'm not saying you can't have both, but it needs to be a discussion. You may lay things out, and Kai decides he doesn't want to live here full time. But you'll never know until you have that conversation."

I sighed deeply. Confrontation was the worst, and I was terrible at it. It's why I did my investigative journalism behind my computer and not out in the field.

"If Kai is what is most important to you," she continued, "some compromises and sacrifices might need to be made. Because that's what you do when you're in a relationship with someone you truly love. Do you see yourself with him long term?"

"Yes, absolutely," I said without hesitation.

"Then there's your answer."

Thirteen

My mother and I continued with some idle chit-chat for another half hour until I heard the front door close. Instantly, I knew I had run out of time.

Kai walked into the kitchen and grinned at my mother, then turned to me. His smile immediately dropped, and that almost made my heart break right there.

"Can we talk?" he asked quietly.

All I could do was nod. With a screech, I scooted my chair away from the table. My mom smiled warmly at the both of us, and I followed Kai up the stairs to my room. He held the door open for me, letting me enter first. Once he had shut it behind him, he leaned against the wood.

Kai sighed deeply. I tried not to fidget and failed miserably. Picking at my fingernails, I couldn't look my boyfriend in the face, afraid I'd see some sort of anger or disappointment. Or worse, there could be a quiet resignation because Kai had decided he no longer wanted to be with me.

"Huck, look at me," he said.

I shook my head. "I'm sorry," I whispered.

Plopping onto my bed, I dropped my head into my hands.

The floor vibrated under my feet as Kai dropped to his knees. He eased his way between my legs and warm hands rubbed soothingly at my thighs.

"Berry..." he said, gently removing my hands from my face. A finger under my chin pushed until my eyes met his. "Please, all I'm asking is that you talk to me. What's going on?"

"This place...I simply don't feel comfortable here. I never have. And I don't know that I ever will. There was a reason I left, and although people might be nice to me *now*, it doesn't mean I can simply forget how they were to me back then. What if it's only a front and things changed if I lived here permanently?"

Kai took my hands and squeezed them to tell me he was here and listening.

"It would be like asking you to move back to your high school where you were bullied," I continued.

His brows pulled together in a frown. "I could live in the same town, though."

"But would you see everyone you went to school with? The ones who mocked you and hurt you, would you see them on a daily basis? Wondering if they still thought of you the same way and were only changing because your father threatened them—" I choked on a sob, unable to continue. But my eyes were already sore from crying, and so I shoved the tears down.

"No," he said softly, understanding dawning. "No, I imagine they'd have moved by now."

I latched on to this and continued, my words becoming more frantic.

"So you see? It's so difficult for me to be around these people every day, and I don't want to do it."

"But, Huck, I think that, given time and some conversations, you'd see that they actually do accept you for who you are. I've been talking with some of them, and they seem genuinely happy that you're home and would like to see you stay. The mayor even approached me and said they had an opening at the newspaper office—I guess they print them out here? But I told him that he should talk to you, because you're honestly more into it than I am. I kind of fell into journalism in college, but it's not something I'm especially passionate about."

"I love my job at the Times," I whispered, aghast. I couldn't believe he was still trying to convince me to stay after all I had told him. "That was a hard position for me to get into. I worked my way through college and took out loans to pay my way, and I had to fight my way up there. I knew nobody, had zero connections, and I still managed to land my dream job. It would be hard for me to simply walk away from that."

"Okay, Berry," Kai said, sounding defeated, his shoulders slumping. No, I didn't want him to be sad about this. I remembered my mother's words—I needed to compromise.

"We could come visit more often," I offered. "Or, hell, even buy a vacation home if you love it so much. But would you really want to move away from your family?"

"You moved away from yours," he countered.

"But you love your family."

"And you don't?" Kai challenged me, staring me down. I swallowed thickly, because of course, he was right. I did love my parents and no, I didn't like being so far from them, without a consistently reliable means of communication. But Kai's parents were used to calling him every few days, having him visit upstate at least twice a month, and they would come to the city almost as often. He couldn't exactly drop off the face of the Earth without them freaking out about it.

I honestly didn't think he would be happy living here full-time, and he wouldn't realize it until he couldn't talk to his parents like normal. Either that, or they would file a missing persons report and when we went to visit, all hell would break loose. No, it'd be easier just to stay in the city.

"You know I love my family, Kai," I said, suddenly exhausted. My head drooped low, and I glanced away from him. This wasn't going well. "But we both know it's a different situation with you and your parents. You cannot simply leave and go somewhere. They'll expect to be able to contact you."

He shrugged. "I could think of some excuse. We're volunteering in the middle of the forest, or something."

I raised a brow at him. "Forever?"

"I didn't say it was a perfect plan," Kai huffed. Now he was getting frustrated with me. Great. This was not going the way I wanted it to.

"Kai," I said, staring at him, *pleading* with him to hear me. "Please."

His face went carefully blank. Any playfulness I usually saw in Kai's eyes was gone. He exhaled roughly, then pushed off my thighs to stand. Running a hand through his hair, Kai looked down upon me.

"Okay," he said. "We'll do things your way. I'm going to take a shower."

I opened my mouth to call to him as he walked away from me, but no sound came out. Did I really want to give in to him so that he'd be happier, even though it would make me miserable? Kai had to realize that moving to The Vale would make me more depressed than normal. It wouldn't be good for me at all. He disappeared into the bathroom and I lost my chance. The door closed between us, and something about it felt final.

Kai would get over it. We could visit more often—maybe not for two weeks at a time, but we could come every couple months. That should hopefully be enough for him. But as the water in the shower began to flow, a small thread of doubt wound its way around my heart.

After our talk, three days were left in our "vacation". Kai was more subdued than usual. He would still smile and laugh with my parents, and converse with the people when we ventured downtown, but he took more solo walks. At night, he slept with his back toward me. Barely spoke to me, except for the bare basics to get through our day.

I hated it.

But I also didn't want to change my mind simply because he was angry with me.

On our last day, we packed our bags in complete silence. My father called for me from downstairs, and I glanced at Kai. He purposefully did not meet my gaze. Holding back a sigh, I placed the shirt I was folding in my suitcase, then walked to the first floor to see what my dad wanted.

Cabbas waited for me in the kitchen, leaning against the counter with his arms crossed. His shirt sleeves were rolled up and his earring sparkled. Sometimes it was difficult to determine what emotion my dad was feeling, or what his mood was. With his Doberman head, his eyes and muzzle didn't portray things the way a more human face would. But I could tell he was disappointed with me.

"Huckleberry," his deep voice rumbled.

"Dad?" I tried not to wince. It was crazy that even as an adult, I was scared of getting in trouble with my parents.

"Your mother told me what has been going on between you and Kai. I might not be an empath like Itsa, but I have noticed the change in the past few days."

Now, I did wince.

"We're just...going through some things," I said weakly.

Cabbas raised a brow. "Son, I only want you to be happy. If that's here or in the human lands, I don't care. Yes, I would love to see you more often, but if The Vale really makes you unhappy, I don't want you here."

I sighed and started to thank him, but my dad held up his hand to stop me.

"However," he continued. "If *Kai* is what makes you happy, you're going to have to do some things that you don't enjoy sometimes if it's what he wants. That's how a relationship works. You won't always be on the same page as each other, but compromises must be made if you want this to last. And over the past two weeks, I can tell you really love him."

"I *am* compromising, Dad," I said. "I promised we could come visit more. Or even buy a little vacation home. But Mom said you knew what was happening to me as a kid, and every time I'm around the townspeople, I feel like

I'm back there. Never knowing how they're going to react to me. Always anticipating an unkind word. Watching intently for any indications in their expression on how our interaction is going to go...It's torturous."

With each word, my dad's posture deflated, and this time I could read the sadness in his expression. Then he stepped forward and wrapped me in a hug. I melted into my father's arms, closing my eyes and squeezing him tight. Cabbas was rarely affectionate with me, and I always treasured these rare moments. He was so much taller than I was that I was completely enveloped in his embrace. Suddenly, I felt like a little kid again, seeking shelter.

Eventually, he pulled me away, holding onto my shoulders and staring me in the eye. "I am forever sorry for how The Vale has treated you. I regret every day that I could not protect you better."

"There was nothing you could do."

"I am your *father*. Of course there was more I could do. I'm sorry, Huckleberry."

My sinuses burned as tears threatened. Cabbas tugged me in for another hug.

"I do hope we'll see you more." His deep voice rumbled in my ear. "I love you, son."

"I love you too, Dad."

An hour later, Kai and I were saying goodbye to my parents. My mother cried as she hugged us both, and my father gave me a *look* that I interpreted to mean, "Remember what we talked about."

Kai smiled sadly at them both, then I opened the portal the same way I had two weeks before, and we stepped through into our living room. Sirens and horns blared outside our window—the sounds of New York City welcoming us home.

Dropping his suitcase down in the middle of the floor, Kai disappeared into our bedroom without a word and closed the door behind him.

Fourteen

Despondency hovered over Kai in a thick cloud. It had been a week since we had returned home, and he'd barely spoken to me.

We went back to work. He was consistently getting reprimanded by our boss, and after three days she'd actually given him a written warning. When we left for the day, he tossed it in the trash, unconcerned. And although he'd never been one to take anything too seriously, Kai had always had a strong work ethic. This wasn't like him at all.

On the subway or in a taxi, he would stare out the window, seemingly lost in his own thoughts. I had tried a few times to snap him out of his reverie but quickly realized that he either didn't want to hear me and so was ignoring me, or I couldn't break through to him.

At home, Kai no longer cooked. I ordered takeout for us every night, but he barely even looked at the food. We sat on the couch watching TV without touching each other. Usually, we'd be squished together, or my head would be in Kai's lap, and he'd play with my hair. Instead, I was cold and walking on eggshells.

I missed my boyfriend.

Which seemed silly because he was *right there*. Always. We lived together. We worked together. We did literally everything together, but Kai was no longer present. I kept waiting for him to return back to his normal self, and he just...wasn't.

That Sunday, I was sitting in a chair, reading a book without actually absorbing any of it. My mood had been dropping steadily each day since we'd been back. But my gaze snapped up with hope when I heard Kai inhale from across the room.

"Huck..." he started. My heart beat faster in anticipation, but Kai didn't continue.

"Yes?" I prompted.

"I'm going to go visit my parents for a bit. I've already informed Elizabeth and I'm leaving tomorrow."

"Oh." I blinked at him. Kai refused to look at me. "Do...do you want me to go with you?"

He shook his head and stood from his seat. "No. I need some space. Plus, I know you're working on a big project right now, and I wouldn't want to take you away from that."

My spirit shattered. Space was never a good thing. I might not have been well-versed in relationships, but it was obvious that when somebody asked for space, it was usually preceding a breakup. The article I was currently writing was an excuse, because Kai knew very well I could work on it remotely.

"Okay," I whispered. "Whatever you need." I hoped that by giving him this, by being there for him—if not physically, then emotionally—he could pull through this fugue.

Kai simply nodded once and disappeared into our bedroom. Several minutes later, he dropped a duffel bag by the front door and flopped onto the couch. When I went to bed, Kai didn't follow. I stayed up well into the night waiting for him, but he never came. Eventually, exhaustion took over, and I slept, but when I awoke, it was to find Kai sleeping on our sofa.

I brushed his hair back gently, admiring his restful face. His eyes fluttered open at my touch, and his face turned ever so slightly into my palm. Then he woke fully, and the dull gaze of the past week stared up at me. What hurt most, though, was the small flinch away from my touch.

"I–I didn't want you to miss your train," I murmured, removing my hand.

Kai checked his phone and swore lightly under his breath. He dressed in record speed while I watched on helplessly. Although he tried to dash out the door, I called out to him and his steps slowed. He continued to face the door, not turning to me.

"I love you," I said.

His head drooped minutely, and his shoulders sagged. Kai took a deep breath.

"I love you, too," he said so quietly I could barely hear him, before he slipped out the door.

The words should have uplifted me, but they did the opposite. Because he had said them so softly. So sadly. Almost like he didn't *want* to love me and was upset that he did. A chill ran through me, and I sank onto the couch, sobbing into my hands.

Four of the worst days of my life dragged past. I would text Kai, but he'd either leave me on read or respond with one or two words only. Once, I tried to call and he forwarded me directly to voicemail. It hurt so much I hadn't done it again.

The apartment was cold, dark, and empty. Devoid of life. I would go to work and muddle my way through my project. Elizabeth yelled at me on Tuesday because I had accidentally merged two projects together, and none of it made sense. I took the verbal lashing, my head hung low as I sat in her well-decorated modern office. She must have felt bad for me, because she finally sighed, told me not to do it again, and let me go home early.

Every day when I got home, I sat on the couch watching mindless TV or doom scrolling on my phone, trying desperately to keep my mind off of Kai. Eventually, I would give up, take a quick shower, and then toss and turn in bed. Sleep evaded me, and when it did find me, I dreamed of Kai. In my mind, he was smiling and laughing. Cooking and singing. Dancing in the kitchen while I watched, grinning madly. Reality would hit me hard and fast when I awoke, reminding me he wasn't there.

On Thursday morning before work I texted him, asking when he'd be home. All he replied with was, "idk."

On Friday, I arrived at work only to find a box on the desk in my cubicle. Within it was a red stapler, a mouse pad with the meme of the dog sitting in fire on it, a few mugs, a succulent, and a photo of Kai with his parents. It was all of Kai's personal effects from his own cubicle. I had gotten him that succulent when his first article was published.

I frowned at the contents, confused. A small knock on the cubicle opening made me jump. Elizabeth stood by my desk, immaculately dressed as always in a pencil skirt, matching blouse, and bright red lipstick. She nodded toward the box.

"I trust you'll be able to get that back to Kai? He said he wouldn't be back and we could throw it out, but I thought he might still want some of it."

"I don't understand," I mumbled.

My boss raised her brows. "He didn't tell you?"

"Tell me what?" I ran a finger over the picture frame. Kai was smiling broadly in the photo with an arm slung around each of his parents. I missed him so much.

"Kai quit. He called me last night to let me know."

He...he quit? Without telling me? Oh God, I had hurt him even more than I'd realized. Tears sprang to my eyes, and I inhaled shakily, trying not to cry at work. Elizabeth tilted her head, observing me.

"Is everything okay?" she asked.

At that moment, I couldn't even think about lying, so I shook my head. She sighed.

"Go home, Huck. You're not going to get any quality work done in this state."

It seemed as if she'd meant it to sound firm, but all I could hear was pity. Still, I nodded and gathered up my things, continuously attempting to keep the tears at bay.

I took a taxi instead of the subway, not wanting multiple pairs of strange eyes on me. It was bad enough the cabbie was seeing me cry in the backseat of his car that smelled like a mixture of B.O. and marijuana.

This had gone far enough. As soon as I got home, I would pack a bag, go upstate, and confront Kai. If he wanted to break up with me, he could do it to my face.

Marching out of the elevator, I threw the door open with more force than was necessary and froze in the entryway. Kai was in the living room. He had a large suitcase at his feet and when he saw me, his face fell. Running a hand through his dark hair, he glanced away from me. My heart raced.

"Kai," I whispered. He blinked rapidly, still facing away from me. I eased into the apartment, gently closing the door behind me. "Kai, please look at me."

With a shuddering inhale, Kai shook his head.

"Please, baby," I pleaded. "Please talk to me. What is going on?"

I recognized Kai had said the exact same words to me only a few weeks before. It felt like I had lived an entire lifetime since we had left The Vale. I took another cautious step toward him.

"You quit your job? And now you're packing. *Please*, Kai, I need to hear it from you. Because my mind has been racing with possibilities and I need to know where we stand."

Finally, Kai glanced up at me. The tears in his eyes instantly made my own water.

"There's nothing to talk about," he said.

"There's *everything* to talk about," I countered. "You've been avoiding me since we got home, and I want to know what you're thinking."

We stood several feet apart, and the distance gnawed at my soul. I wanted nothing more than to fall into his arms and feel his warmth surrounding me. Kai was my home. My safe place. I was lost without him.

Kai huffed a laugh and ran his hand through his hair again.

"If you had been listening to me at all," he said, "you'd know why I've been upset."

I frowned and dared another step forward. Kai stayed rooted in place.

"Kai, please help me understand," I begged.

"This is just it, Huck," he said, gesturing between the two of us. "You haven't been fucking listening to me. When I tried to have a conversation with you about living in The Vale, you shut down. You wouldn't even try to compromise with me."

Confusion rattled through me. "I did, though. I said we could visit more often or get a vacation home over there. I want you to be happy too, Kai."

"Do you?" His dark eyes flashed with anger. He'd never looked at me that way, and my stomach dropped. "Because you steamrolled the entire conversation before we could talk it through completely. You simply put your foot down, and that was that. It feels like your work means more to you than I do."

My jaw slackened. "That's not true at all! And besides, it's important work."

Kai sighed deeply. "It is, and I never said otherwise. I only wanted you to think about me instead of your job when we talked about where to live. Especially when I could see how miserable you were every time you were in that office. *Especially* since most of your work can be done remotely."

I shook my head, disbelieving that Kai could be so upset with me over this.

"Why does it matter where we live as long as we're together?" I asked.

"Exactly."

Silence hung heavy between us. Kai and I stared at each other, and my chest felt tight. This wasn't at all how I'd imagined our relationship. I honestly thought we'd be together for the rest of our lives.

"So, what are you saying?" I whispered, exhausted.

A hand that I'd held in my own more times than I could count ran through hair that I'd sifted through my fingers each night. A sigh escaped lips I had kissed. Lips I knew intimately. And eyes that had stared into mine with love and adoration now gazed at me dully.

"I can't do this anymore, Huck. I'm sorry."

He picked up his suitcase and walked around me toward the front door. I said nothing. My tongue was glued to the roof of my overly dry mouth, and all I could do was watch the man I loved leave my life.

Kai stopped in the doorway with another sigh. Without looking back at me, he said, "You can stay in the apartment. Rent is paid up for the next six months."

Then he was gone.

I crumpled to the ground, my legs no longer able to support me. Shivers racked my body, and quiet tears flowed down my face.

Rent is paid up for the next six months.

Even though he was angry with me...even though he broke up with me, Kai continued to take care of me. He knew I couldn't afford to live here on my own, and this gave me time to find another solution.

A sob ripped out of my throat at the thought. I curled into a ball on the cold floor and cried myself to sleep.

Fifteen

I spent the weekend drifting between my bed and the shower. When I felt restless, I'd pace in the living room.

The TV was off, no music played, and nobody was singing in the kitchen. The only sounds were those of the city and my own sobs. I kept my phone nearby in the hope that Kai would call me. Tell me it was all a big mistake, and he took it back. He didn't actually want to leave me. But he never did.

I lost count of how many times I opened our text thread to send him a message, then lost my nerve. If he wanted to talk to me, he would. I needed to respect his wishes.

By Sunday morning, I couldn't take it any longer. I opened Kai's dresser drawer, hoping he'd left a shirt behind. Maybe enveloping myself in his scent would help. Realistically, it would only hurt more, but I needed to feel close to him. Just for a bit.

There were no clothes left, but in the middle of the drawer sat a little box. Its exterior was a black velvet, which was soft as I gingerly touched it. I knew what it was, but I needed to look, anyway. Popping open the box, my stomach dropped. And fresh tears filled my eyes and sinuses, even though I thought I had cried myself out.

Inside, the box was lined with a smooth white silk, and in its center was a ring. With trembling fingers, I pulled it free and dropped the box. The metal was cold to the touch but warmed as I inspected it. The edges were silver, but the middle of the ring was a gorgeous polished wood. It had red, orange, and yellow tones—all my favorite autumnal colors.

And my heart broke anew as I slipped it onto my left ring finger. It fit perfectly.

It hit me in that moment—exactly how much of a fool I'd been. All Kai wanted was for me to *listen* to him, and I couldn't even manage that. He had wanted me to marry him, and I'd thrown it all away.

God, I was such an idiot.

Wallowing would get me nowhere. Resolved, I threw some clothes into a backpack and texted Elizabeth that I was taking a few mental health days, then turned my phone off so I wouldn't have to deal with the backlash.

I waved down a taxi at the curb below our building and nervously bounced my knee the entire drive to the train station.

Usually, I enjoyed the slow amble of train rides, but not that day. My leg continued to jump restlessly, and soon the other joined as well. Next, I gnawed on my lower lip. Then

I was picking at my nails, scratching phantom itches, and generally behaving like a live ball of anxiety.

My stomach erupted in butterflies when we pulled into the station in upstate New York that was closest to Kai's parents' house.

An Uber drove me the rest of the way to the estate, which took close to another hour. By the time we arrived at the massive iron gates, I was nervousness personified. The driver peered at me in the rearview mirror, worry written on his face. He was a kind, middle-aged man and had a picture of himself, his wife, and two teenage kids pinned to his air-conditioning vent. At the beginning of the journey, he'd attempted to make small talk but soon realized I wasn't in the right headspace for it. Instead, he turned on some calming classical music and snuck peeks at me periodically.

"Do you want me to wait here?" he asked.

I shook my head. "No, that's okay. I'll get out here and push the buzzer for the gate." Now I was mad I'd never learned the code. I would have to convince someone to let me in.

"You sure, kid? We're kind of in the middle of nowhere up here."

Just in case, I checked to see if I had cell service. It was only 4G, but it would be enough to hire another ride if this went sideways. I didn't really want this nice man to watch me get rejected.

"I'm sure. Thank you for the ride."

"Good luck, kid."

Exiting the car, I closed the door behind me and winced at the sound echoing off the trees. The vegetation here was different than in The Vale. Kai's parents had surrounded their mansion with evergreens that could withstand the fall and winter. But I found myself missing the boardwalk through the forest and the leaves crinkling under my feet.

I wished I could talk to my mom about all of this. She would give me sage advice, hug me, and make me a cup of tea. My father would give his own gruff thoughts as he sat at the table with us. I missed them.

With a jolt, I realized...I missed *The Vale*.

But not The Vale I had grown up in. I longed for the one where Kai was with me. Showing him around and spending time with him there had changed it for the better. He helped me rewrite my memories of the town. Instead of remembering people spitting at my feet in the town square, I saw myself dancing under the fairy lights with Kai. The riverbank where a group of kids once pushed me under was now where Kai and I were caught making out.

He'd completely changed The Vale for me, and I hadn't listened to him when he tried to tell me it was different. Everyone *had* been nicer to me. Some strange looks, sure, but nobody had been outright mean or derogatory the way they used to be. Maybe people were capable of change.

Maybe I could change too.

Gravel crunched behind me as my ride drove off, and I tentatively approached the coded gate box. I pushed the red call button and waited.

A crackle made me almost jump out of my skin, and a woman's slightly accented voice emanated from the speaker.

"Huck?"

I cleared my throat. "Hi, Mrs. Miyashiro. Uh, is Kai home?"

A pause. If he wasn't here, I had no Plan B.

"He is," she said hesitantly, and I breathed a sigh of relief. "But I don't know if it's a good idea for you to be here."

"Please," I begged. "I only want to talk to him for a minute."

"Who is it?" a male voice said. I sucked in a breath, but recognized him as Kai's dad, Sato.

"Huckleberry," Naomi said, her voice sounding slightly farther away.

"Let him in," Sato said. Their voices were muffled, and I unabashedly pressed my ear to the speaker so I could hear better.

"Are you sure that's a good idea?"

"I've never seen our son happier than when he was with Huck, and I've never seen him more miserable than he is now."

Simultaneously, my heart soared and shattered.

"Are you still there?" Naomi's voice was loud in my ear, and I jolted backward, my pulse racing.

"Yes," I said, waiting and holding my breath.

"We're going to let you in," she said, then hurried to continue, "*but* if he doesn't want you here, you'll have to leave."

"Absolutely," I promised. "After this, if Kai doesn't want to see me again, I will leave and never come back. I promise."

It would kill me, but I would do it.

A beep sounded and the gates swung open with a metallic creak. I started the long trek up the paved road lined with cypress trees. It should be illegal to have a driveway of this length. Or there at least should be a golf cart waiting to transport people to the house. Although most people came here by car and not on foot.

By the time I reached the front of the house, I was panting and a sheen of sweat covered my brow. The door swung open, and I struggled to compose myself. Naomi Miyashiro was well put together, as always, with not a single hair out of place. In contrast, I must have appeared like a half-drowned city rat.

I straightened my shirt out, wiped my forehead, and patted down my hair—which was back to its dyed light brown color.

"Come in," Naomi said, stepping aside. "He's up in his bedroom."

The house was gigantic, and she had to show me the way to Kai's bedroom on the third floor. She rapped gently on his door once we arrived.

"Kai," she called softly. "There's someone to see you."

There was a soft clatter on the other side of the room. Kai spoke—his words muffled by the walls. "Who would be here to see—" He pulled open his door and stopped short.

Oxygen stalled in my lungs. He was gorgeous. Dressed only in loose-fitting pajama pants and a tank top, Kai's dark hair was mussed and slightly wet from a shower. I had seen him dressed formally and casually, in a suit and in a shirt made entirely of mesh, in everything and nothing. But this...this was my favorite version of him.

I smiled—although it probably appeared more of a grimace—and waved awkwardly.

"Hi," I mumbled.

Kai stared at his mom with something like betrayal flashing behind his eyes. Naomi winced with guilt.

"I'll give you two a minute," she said, then hustled away.

We both watched her leave, and as she rounded the corner, Kai ran a hand through his hair. He sighed deeply.

"You might as well come in," he said, and held the door open for me.

I eased around him, carefully avoiding touching him in any way. If I felt his skin against mine, I would lose any sense of courage I currently possessed. With a *snick*, we were alone.

Kai brushed past me, sitting on his bed. Shoulders slumped forward, he glanced up at me, appearing exhausted. I stood in the middle of his lavish bedroom, fidgeting. Shifting from one foot to the other. My eyes darted around the room, and I had the distinct unease of not knowing what to do with my hands.

"You came all the way up here?" Kai asked.

I could only nod. Something brightened in his gaze before dimming again.

"Might as well say what you want," he continued.

"I—" I started, then stopped to clear my throat. "Kai, I'm sorry. I'm so sorry. You're absolutely right; I wasn't listening to you."

His eyes widened a fraction, but he didn't say anything, so I rambled on.

"You were trying to find a solution that was best for *both* of us, and I was only thinking of myself. I was terrified of living in The Vale, but that's not an excuse for my selfish behavior. And I can see now that people were treating me better than they had in the past. I just didn't want to acknowledge it. I didn't know how.

"But I do know you make me into the best version of myself, Kai. I am happiest when I'm with you, and if I've driven you away from me, I'll have to live with that. For the rest of my life, I will remember our time together fondly."

I fell to my knees in front of him and gazed into those dark eyes I used to call home.

"I was so, so wrong to dismiss you before, and I would give *anything* to take it back. These past couple of weeks have been the worst of my life. I was stupid. And foolish."

From my pocket, I pulled out the small box I'd found in Kai's drawer. He inhaled sharply at the sight of it. I twisted it in my hands and stared at the black velvet. Whatever Kai's expression was, I knew I couldn't look at him. It would break me.

"You had always understood. We had similar childhoods and I wanted to believe my experience was different—unique—simply because I had grown up around creatures instead of humans. But that's not true at all. You are acutely aware of how mean people can be simply because you're different."

I reached my hand out to touch Kai's knee but thought better of it and pulled away. Finally, I glanced up at him to see tears swimming in his eyes. My sinuses burned at the sight. I'd been able to fight off crying this entire time, but watching Kai break would be my undoing.

"All this is to say," I continued, my voice wavering. "I love you. I love you so much, and I will be forever sorry that I drove this wedge between us. I don't care where we live. I don't care what I do with my life, or where I work. All I want is *you*, Kai. You're all I need. Everything else will fall into place as long as you're by my side."

Words failed me and I stopped talking. I had laid it all out—bared my soul—and now it was up to Kai to decide.

"What are you asking?" Kai whispered.

"Can you forgive me?" A tear slipped down my cheek. "Please, Kai. Please, baby, forgive me and take me back. I miss you so damn much."

Kai dropped off his bed and landed on his knees in front of me. Shaking hands gently cupped my face, and we both cried together. Kai brushed the moisture off my face with his thumbs.

"*Fuck*," Kai said. "I missed you too, Berry."

Then he was kissing me. His lips tasted like salt and heaven combined, and I melted into his touch. I wrapped my arms around his neck to draw him in closer. For several minutes, we lost ourselves in each other, and my soul sang at Kai's nearness. It felt like coming home, and I vowed I would never do anything to jeopardize our relationship again.

Eventually, we stopped kissing, and Kai rested his brow against mine.

"I love you," I whispered.

"I love you, too," Kai said. His hand wrapped around mine and stole the box I'd forgotten I was holding. "I think I'll hold onto this for a bit. If that's okay with you."

My stomach dipped. "Anything you want, Kai. Anything at all."

When he kissed me again, I knew we would be okay. We would persevere. And I would do everything in my power to make sure it stayed that way.

Sixteen

Three months later, I was putting the finishing touches on our new mantle. Warm arms wrapped around my waist, and I leaned back into Kai's embrace. He placed a soft kiss on my neck.

"It looks good," he said.

"Thank you." I ran my fingers along his arm and watched goosebumps trail in their wake. Kai kissed me again. Turning, I ran my hands up his chest and behind his neck, rising on my toes to kiss his lips.

The weight of the ring on my left hand was still new but felt right. We had discussed taking things slowly. But we had spent every moment together since reconciling, and I had woken up each day wanting to ask Kai to marry me. I knew I needed to take things at his pace, though, because I was the one who had hurt him.

And just last week, we bought a house. Kai had tried to carry me over the threshold but stumbled, and we both almost crashed to the floor. Luckily, he managed to catch most of his balance so that it was a slow fall, and we lay on the hardwood floor laughing hysterically. Once we had calmed down, Kai glanced over at me. Interlacing our fingers, he brought my hand to his mouth and an air of seriousness dropped over us.

For a moment, I panicked. But his gaze was full of love, longing, and hope. With his other hand, he pulled out that little velvet box and flipped it open.

"Huckleberry Silverwater-Raad," he said reverently. "Will you marry me?"

I wrinkled my nose. "Only if I can take your last name."

Kai smiled widely. "Deal."

He rolled on top of me, and we worshiped each other in our very own home. When we were spent and sweaty, Kai slipped the ring onto my finger.

A knock on our front door had us hastily pulling on clothing and smoothing down our hair. But when I opened it to find my mother on the other side, her smirk told me she knew exactly what had just happened. Pink stained my cheeks as I blushed, but she only patted my face affectionately and handed me a pot of peach-colored verbenas.

My dad followed her inside, and his nose sniffed. My flush deepened because I knew what his more sensitive sense of smell could detect. Although his lip twitched, Cabbas said nothing, only clapping me on the shoulder hard enough to buckle my knees.

"Proud of you, son," he rumbled. My soul lifted at the words.

That was the best day of my life.

After I had found Kai at his parent's house, we had talked well into the night. I admitted that I did actually miss The Vale. Every other time I had visited after I moved away, I had only stayed at my parents' house, and only for a few days. I'd never gone out and seen anybody. Kai had forced me out of my bubble, and it allowed me to see a better side of the town.

I told him I wanted to move back.

He had been unsure at first. I loved him all the more for it. Because I had such a strong reaction when he first brought it up, he didn't want me to move only because he did. I explained my reasoning to him, but he made me sit on it for a month. When I told him I hadn't changed my mind, we made little trips back and forth while we hunted for houses.

Finally, we found the perfect one. A little two-bedroom cottage near my parents, but on the edge of the forest. Our backyard opened into the trees, and our closest neighbors were far enough away that we couldn't see or hear them.

Now, we were completely moved in.

I told Elizabeth that I would be going part time at work. Meaning I'd be in the office only two days per week, and working remotely the rest of the time. Really, I'd probably still be working full-time hours, but it would have to be less until we figured out the internet situation.

Apparently, Dave had been working on getting Wi-Fi and cell service to The Vale. Who knew Mothman would be such a tech guru?

My parents, Kai, and I had petitioned Mayor Thunderhoof for a semi-permanent portal permit. He'd been hesitant, concerned that going back and forth so often would give humans more of an opportunity to accidentally stumble upon The Vale. But we reassured him that I would use Kai's room in his parents' city apartment for moving back and forth. It was a penthouse in an expensive building and therefore well-guarded. He eventually relented and gave me the permit.

Speaking of Kai's parents, we had debated for weeks about what we would tell them. After consulting with Itsa and Cabbas, we decided to simply tell them the truth. We brought them over to The Vale one night to have dinner with my parents. Naomi and Sato had gawked at first, but after thirty minutes—and a bit of wine—they had been smiling and laughing with the rest of us. It had been their idea for me to use their apartment for travel and had gotten me registered with security at the front desk so I could come and go as I pleased.

After living in The Vale for a few months, when the cherry blossoms were blooming, Kai and I began to be approached by teens and young adults who wanted to visit the human lands but didn't know how. Melissa and only a few others had ever made the trip and were tight-lipped about how they'd done it.

For obvious reasons, the kids' parents were wary about letting them leave. But Kai worked with Dave and Mayor Thunderhoof and developed something of an ambassador program. Interested creatures would apply and there was a rigorous interview process. Once approved, the mayor would give them a temporary portal permit, and Dave would fashion a glamour that could make any creature—no matter what combination of body parts they had—appear completely human.

Kai would accompany them into the human lands and get them settled in college, or at a job for some of the older applicants. He'd take them shopping for human clothes, teach them slang, and generally make sure they wouldn't stand out *too* much. Then, he would periodically check in on them and help with any needs they might have. The work was extremely fulfilling for Kai, and it allowed him time to visit his parents often, which they all appreciated.

I rekindled (platonic) friendships with both Dave and Thad, and the four of us would spend time together often. It even seemed like something was brewing between the centaur and Mothman, but they weren't saying anything about it. Kai and I would steal knowing glances at all the slightly-too-casual-to-be-casual touches. It was cute.

Not a single day went by that I wasn't happy with our choice. Kai and I would wake up in the morning in our shared bed and have a cup of coffee on our back patio. We'd go about our respective work for the day, eat dinner together, and fall asleep in each other's arms. It was pure bliss. And I could do it every single day for the rest of my life.

Epilogue

Kai

It had been close to a year since Huck and I had moved to The Vale, and the trees had turned colors again. The forest behind our little home was awash with maroon, burnt orange, and gold. A slight chill in the air made us huddle underneath the blankets Huck crocheted and gave us an excuse to cuddle close—not that we needed one.

We both were well established in our positions, and since Dave had figured out a way to get us the internet, Huck had been staying home more and going to the city less. Still, he had written a brilliant exposé on that dirty politician, which actually uncovered some illegal activities, and Podolski was now sitting behind bars. Berry had practically glowed for a week after he heard the news.

So far with my own ambassador role, I'd helped almost two dozen creatures find a place within the human lands.

It was rewarding work, seeing them thrive in a new environment.

Together, we realized we were well-established within our home, our relationship, and The Vale in general, and decided to get married. Initially, we had planned on a quiet ceremony with only family and close friends, but Thad was terrible at keeping secrets. He'd insisted on making us an extravagant wedding cake, then bragged about it to every single patron who walked into his shop.

We'd been a little annoyed at first until it became clear the citizens of The Vale were all genuinely happy for us and simply wanted to celebrate our love. Once we acknowledged that, how could we say no? The intimate wedding quickly became a large spectacle, but we refused to move the location.

I married the love of my life surrounded by trees, singing birds, and tearful family members. Loud cheers erupted when we kissed and sealed ourselves together. A band played for us in the town's gazebo, and we danced the night away. I couldn't take my eyes off Huck; he looked so handsome in the suit I'd had tailored for him. Soon enough, I couldn't take it anymore, and I stole him away to our home where I showed him with my lips and fingers just how much I loved him.

I would forever be grateful that Huck had the courage that day to travel halfway across New York State to apologize and tell me he loved me. I had been miserable without him, but I didn't want to reach out only to be hurt again. When he *showed* me he realized he'd been wrong, and he made the necessary changes, I knew I couldn't live if he wasn't by my side. A little dramatic, sure, but my love for him ran deep into my bones and through my entire soul.

As I stared into his adoring blue eyes, I knew my Berry felt the same, and we could spend forever exactly where we were meant to be. Together.

THE END

Acknowledgements

Thank you to:

Morgan—for always being there for me, creating this stunning cover (and chapter headers and scene breaks), and for alpha reading.

Sarah—best proofreader and cheerleader ever. Love being able to call you a friend, even if we've only met online.

John—for always supporting me when I get crazy ideas and wear myself thin.

The random Tumblr post that spawned this crazy idea.

And to all of my readers. Thank you so much for following along with me, Huck, and Kai. I appreciate you more than you know.

(If this is the first of my books that you've read, please don't expect the others to be similar. They are not.)

About the Author

Jeannin Counts is a physician assistant, avid reader, and devoted soccer mom, minivan and all. A lifelong nerd, she has collected many eclectic hobbies over the years and has always wanted to put her broad range of knowledge to use as a writer.

When she isn't caring for patients or at her writing desk, Jeannin can be found relishing new culinary adventures, exploring the lost arts of candle making and ballroom dancing, or simply nestled up with a good book. If you hear her shouting, it's just the TV (go Dolphins!).

Jeannin resides in California with her spouse and two young sons.

Also by Jeannin

Celestial Whispers series:

Secrets and Stardust
Deceit and Darkness
Between Stars and Salvation